THE MURDERS OF THE MOONLIGHT LADIES

A Maxwell Graham Mystery Thriller

Lawrence Falcetano

THE MURDERS OF THE MOONLIGHT LADIES
A Maxwell Graham Mystery Thriller

First Edition

"A man's face is his autobiography.
A woman's face is her work of fiction."
—Oscar Wilde

"The death of a beautiful woman is,
unquestionably, the most poetical
topic in the world."
—Edgar Allan Poe

—To my sons: Christopher and Jason,

with love and gratitude —

CHAPTER 1

I had shut down my computer and was about to leave for the day when my desk phone rang. Chief Briggs wanted me in his office. Connecting with Briggs this late in the day meant something couldn't wait until tomorrow and usually accompanied a discussion with which I wouldn't be happy.

Briggs was sitting in his swivel chair behind his desk, tapping the keys on his laptop when I entered. Without looking up, he said, "Sit."

I could see he had been working on something important by the way he furrowed his brow, then examined the screen to reaffirm the correctness of what he had just written. He was wearing a short-sleeved white shirt with the collar button open. His tie and suit jacket were hanging on the back of his chair. Although his office was cool, there was a hint of glistening perspiration on his forehead and his face appeared flush, contrasting against his gray hair and mustache, causing them to appear lighter than they were.

I slid into one of the visitor's chairs and waited while he tapped out a few more sentences.

Briggs' office was the largest in the bureau. *The privileges of rank.* A large mahogany desk sat in front of three windows that looked out onto 35th Street. A high-back leather chair into which Briggs could park his huge frame partnered the desk. Two visitor chairs sat in front of it all. The desktop was orderly and functional: a phone bank, a laptop, a rotating pen holder, and several framed photographs of his daughter and grandchildren. Framed documents hung on a side wall, attesting to Briggs' academic achievements and the many awards he had received during his long police career. A water cooler, one potted floor plant, and a metal filing cabinet completed the furnishings.

When he finished, Briggs closed his laptop, swiveled his chair around, removed a file folder from his desk drawer, and dropped it on the desk in front of me. On the top right corner of the front cover, I read the typewritten words: MOONLIGHT LADIES, INC.

"Are you familiar with that name?" he said.

The title didn't ring a bell, but because of the peculiarity of the name, it had somehow buried itself in my memory. Maybe I'd read it in a report or someone had mentioned it in conversation.

"Sounds like a female vocal group," I said.

"It's an escort service here in midtown."

"A prostitution case?" I said. "The last time I checked, we were homicide."

When it came to police work, Briggs came right to the point. "Somebody is killing the Moonlight Ladies," he said. "Three murders in as many months."

"Three for three," I said.

I reminded myself there are no coincidences in police work.

"It's a legit service, owned and operated by a guy named Hayden Benning; no criminal record and no citations against the company in its five-year existence."

"Until now," I said.

"I've had McClusky and Garcia on it, but they haven't come up with much."

"Homicides take time to solve," I said.

"Time is what I don't have," Briggs said. "The media's gotten a hold of it and is having a field day. They're already creating the false narrative of a serial killer running amuck in the city."

"Sensationalism sells newspapers," I said. "Mundane truths don't."

"The truth is, the Mayor's having a shitfit. The city council is on his back and he's on mine. They don't want to start a panic by having people believe there's a maniac loose. The mayor wants this case pursued aggressively. I'm working on my report to him now, explaining this department's intentions and accomplishments—which aren't many."

Mike Briggs ran the detective bureau by his own rules. He was as hard as nails and strictly by the book, yet maintained an understanding and compassion few in his position possessed. Because of his hard-nosed approach to criminal justice, opinions of him varied but were more favorable among the officers who served under him than his superiors. Despite his rough reputation, any cop that was a part of his team found him to be a friend.

"What've you got for me?" I said.

"The mayor wants my best man on this. And he wants quick action. That means you. Don't let that go to your head," he added."

"I'll have to wrap up the cases I'm working on," I said.

"Give them to McClusky. His up-to-date report is in that file. It's not much, but it's a place for you to start."

Briggs turned back to his laptop, opened the screen, and began tapping the keys again. Intense concentration returned to his face. Our conversation was over.

He had given me the case with his acclamation that I was his *best man*. Now I'd have to live up to his praise. I picked up the folder and said, "I'll get right on it, chief."

He didn't hear me or chose not to. I closed his office door behind me and left.

***

My drive to work the next morning had been as uncomfortable as my drive home; the mercury at 9:00 a.m. was already pushing eighty. That New York City summer had been hotter than usual, with temperatures hovering in the low nineties for a month and the humidity so thick it felt like maple syrup against your skin. Air conditioners droned on throughout the city, creating the sound of invading locusts and testing Con Ed's ability to keep up with the demand. People splashed in backyard pools and packed metro area beaches like sardines in oil, seeking a respite from the unrelenting heat, but gaining only temporary relief.

That morning, I was dressed for the onslaught of heat. A short-sleeved button-down shirt, open at the collar, summer khakis, and a pair of casual shoes. I had shed the suit and tie earlier in the summer; much to the disfavor of Chief Briggs. He preferred his investigators to present a professional appearance.

If the AC unit in my Chevy Nova hadn't crapped out on me, my shirt wouldn't have been plastered to my back with sweat. As I walked into the bureau, the AC hit me like a bucket of ice chips. It felt good, despite the chill that wiggled up my spine.

The Midtown Manhattan precinct building is on West 35th Street. The detective bureau comprises desks placed in a series of rows in one large room. Each detective had been assigned to his or her desk according to seniority. The most senior occupied a desk with a window view. By my request, I had been relegated to a far corner of the room, flanked by two windows, a location out of earshot and much to my satisfaction.

I was eager to read McClusky's file. But my first stop was to my partner, Danny Nolan, to fill him in about our new assignment.

Danny was reading off his computer screen as I approached. Without looking away, he pointed to two cups of coffee on his desk. I took one, removed the lid, and blew into it to cool it down. Danny turned his computer off, reached for his coffee, and waited to hear what I had to say.

I sipped my coffee, scrunched up my face and said, "Sweet, Lord! I don't take sugar."

Danny said, "You've got mine."

As we exchanged cups, I said, "New assignment. One of special interest to Briggs."

Danny took a drink of his coffee, screwed his face up, put the lid on the cup, and dropped it into his wastebasket. "Why so special?" he said.

"Someone's killing the moonlight, ladies. The heat from city hall is on Briggs."

I waited for Danny to ask *who* or *what* is the moonlight ladies, instead, he said, "I know the name."

"Then you've used their services?" I said.

"Do I look like I need to pay for companionship?" he said. He ran his fingers through his wavy black hair and straightened his tie in a facetious gesture of self-absorbed conceit.

Danny was no master of levity, but he had all the qualities that made him a good cop. He was humble, hardworking, and conscientious, and possessed an unwavering dedication to police work. A suit and tie were his on the job attire (regardless of temperature) unless an undercover assignment called for a change of wardrobe. His two preoccupations were his career and finding a wife, not necessarily in that order. Despite the disparity in our ages, we enjoyed mutual respect. He for my professional experience and me for his youthful exuberance and dedication to his profession. Under my auspices, he had become a friend and partner I could trust and rely on.

I gave him a perplexing look when he offered me his smile, then I put the lid back on my coffee cup and dropped it into the wastebasket with his.

I said, "Too weak. Too sweet. Too bitter."

He said, "Maybe you should start drinking tea."

I said, "Maybe you should find a new barista."

At my desk, I powered up my laptop and checked my email. Nothing needed my immediate attention, so I opened my checkbook and wrote the monthly check to my ex-wife, Marlene. I'd been late with the check once or twice, but Marlene hadn't made a big deal of it. An electronic transfer would have made things easier for us both, but I wasn't comfortable with it. Despite the convenience, the process made me feel like Marlene was *taking* rather than I was *giving*.

Marlene wanted out of our marriage after nineteen years. I guess I was too busy or too stupid to see it coming. There were years of shift work and weekend work and postponed vacations that had stretched her tolerance to the limit. And she'd suffered the daily uncertainty of whether her husband would come home each day in one piece or come home at all. Our union produced two beautiful daughters, and we loved each other as much as any married couple could. But near the end, the bickering and complaining took their toll on me and I conceded to the divorce. No one was to blame. Marlene had the marriage, and I had the career and sometimes it's difficult to balance both.

We had become bitter divorce adversaries but came to the mutual agreement that civil behavior was the better way to go for the sake of our two daughters.

Christie and Justine smiled out at me from the framed photograph on my desk. I smiled back at them each morning before I started my work day. The rigors of raising my daughters surpassed anything I'd experienced in my police career. It's a labor of love I don't regret. Since Marlene bought the house at the Jersey shore, I missed them every day. I had visitation rights, every Monday and Wednesday and every other weekend. I tried to stay included in their lives, but it wasn't easy with my uneven schedule. I saw my daughters whenever I could.

I slid the check into an envelope, sealed it, and put it in my outgoing box. Then I removed McClusky's report from my desk drawer and open it to the first page. It began with a transcript of McClusky's interview with Hayden Benning.

Benning was forty-six, born and raised in Utica, New York. He'd attended NYU business school after having served four years in the United States Navy. After his service, he and a naval buddy, Mike Ellison, started the escort agency. Ellison had been discharged early from the service due to experiencing a form of PTSD. He had been married and living with his wife in a rented house in Bay Ridge, Brooklyn, when he hooked up with Benning. Two years after he and Benning started the business, Ellison took his own life, leaving Benning the sole owner/operator of the Moonlight Ladies. The business had a shaky beginning, but over the years had developed and maintained a solid reputation as a legitimate company throughout the Tri-State area. The agency had no improprieties until the murders.

The addresses of the women that worked at the agency were listed next to their names. A second list contained the names of those currently employed. Each current employee's history has a thumbnail photograph stapled to it. I counted a dozen names.

On the third page, I referred to the interview between Detective McClusky and Benning, and I got the feeling—by Benning's choice of words—that he was being evasive. McClusky's footnote stated he felt the same about the conversation. I'd find out for myself by interviewing Hayden Benning first. I needed to know who he was. Words on paper don't reveal much. It was like taking an interview by phone. It doesn't work. You can learn more from a person by seeing them close up. I preferred to see Benning close up, feel his vibes, read his body language, and smell his aftershave. Lies and deceit don't always come out of one's mouth. But are revealed through facial expressions, body language, and a person's general attitude. Good detective work requires face to face interviewing.

The last page of the report contained the details of the crime victims. The first was Marianne Williamson, a twenty-seven-year-old from upstate New York. She worked for the agency for two years before being murdered. With credentials like that, I wondered why she hadn't found work in her chosen profession and how she came to be employed at Moonlight

Ladies. She was found strangled to death in her apartment on Central Park West.

The second victim was a thirty-one-year-old Asian woman named Kimi Nakamura (Kim to her friends). Her thumbnail photo showed a beautiful woman with satin black hair and pearl black eyes that seemed to float off the photograph. She had been the owner/operator of a string of high-end beauty salons but when the business fell on hard times; she liquidated her debt and sold the franchise. Like Marianne Williamson, she had found work at Moonlight Ladies. She was strangled to death behind the steering wheel of her Porsche.

A third victim was Adele Rodgers a twenty-two-year-old honor student and graduate of Vassar College who had been working for moonlight ladies temporarily. She met her death in her Brooklyn Heights apartment. Strangled like the others.

All three crimes took place within three months of each other. None of the women had been with an escort for a week before they were killed. The investigations remained open. To date, there are no suspects. Other than these women having worked for Moonlight Ladies, there had to be a common denominator connecting their murders. Finding it would be a challenge.

Chapter 2

The office of Moonlight Ladies was on the third floor of the Hartwood Building on Fifth Avenue in Manhattan. I phoned Hayden Benning and set up a two o'clock interview. During our conversation, he'd made it a point to mention he had told the police everything he knows but will answer my questions if it helped further the case. Offering that statement again suggested reticence, but I might have been wrong.

I arrived on Fifth Avenue by one-forty. I couldn't find a parking space, so I parked by a hydrant and walked across the street to the Hartwood Building. My Chevy Nova looked out of place parked on Fifth Avenue. Its faded paint, missing hubcaps, and strategically placed strips of duct tape conflicted with the opulence of modern-day high-end vehicles that were conventional to the Avenue.

The Chevrolet Nova was the first family car Marlene and I had purchased during our marriage. It had served our family well, with commutes to school, church, grocery shopping, and other assorted lifetime travels. The old gal had been a family member for a long time. After our divorce, Marlene kept the Audi. I got the Nova.

The main lobby of the Hartwood Building was a vast octagon-shaped enclosure with a cathedral ceiling. Its perimeter was dotted with boutiques and coffee shops and ornamented with brass and glass. I chose one of the four elevators that were available and rode up to the third floor. When the elevator doors opened, I started down a long corridor, whose walls were decorated with more brass and glass. I reached a pair of polished cherry wood doors at the end of the corridor upon which shiny brass letters announced: MOONLIGHT LADIES, INC. COME IN.

I opened a door and went in.

I stepped into a posh reception/waiting area. Its walls were painted a soft mauve with the brass and glass motive carried through to the furnishings. A horseshoe-shaped reception desk stood in one corner, while a white leather sofa and chairs occupied the opposite side of the room. Potted plants placed strategically about gave the room a tropical ambiance. A stack of magazines was spread atop a glass kidney-shaped coffee table. One wall was adorned with framed portraits of the most beautiful women I had ever seen. The photos had been hung in horizontal rows of ten; each woman smiled with breathtaking beauty into the camera.

I approached a young woman seated behind the desk who was as attractive as the framed beauties displayed on the wall. She was what one might call pretty, not beautiful. Her black shoulder length hair contrasted against her peach colored complexion and dimpled cheeks. Her overall appearance was one of innocent charm. I showed her my shield and said, "Detective Max Graham. I have a two o'clock with Mr. Benning."

She ran a delicate finger down a list on her computer screen, then said, "I'm sorry. I don't have you on the list. What was the name again?"

I said, "Graham, like the crackers."

I could see she had no idea what I meant, but it was worth the try.

"Did you say you were a detective?" she said.

"I did," I said.

"I thought detectives were scruffy-looking guys who smoked cigars and wore wrinkled rain coats."

"We are," I said. "I dress this way when I'm undercover."

She raised her eyebrows and said, "Undercover. That sounds exciting."

I said, "It is. You should see my fake nose and eye glass disguise."

She gave me a sidelong look and a half-smile. "Now you're kidding with me," she said.

When I offered her a wink and a reassuring grin, she said, "I'll let Mr. Benning know you're here. Have a seat. He'll be with you shortly."

I thanked her and made myself comfortable in one of the leather chairs and engrossed myself in a magazine to ease the boredom of wait time. I was the only one in the room, other than the framed beauties smiling down from the wall behind me. The occasional ringing of the phone and the litany of "Moonlight Ladies. Can I help you?" were the only things interrupting the silence. After thirty minutes, Hayden Benning decided he had time to see me; so much for my two o'clock appointment.

Benning's office was as elaborately designed as the outer office. Lots of brass and glass again. A wall of arch-top windows offered a view onto Fifth Avenue, in front of which was situated a large cherry wood desk. On the desk, there were two laptops, one on either end. A brass and chrome combination, telephone, and intercom were within easy reach. In a high-back leather chair, Hayden Benning sat with a genial smile as he watched me enter his office. He was as handsome as the women that worked for him were beautiful. When he stood, I guessed him to be about my height, an even six feet. He was deeply tanned and his blond hair was neatly combed and barbered. The thin blond mustache he cultivated gave him that 1940s look. His suit looked like an Armani, expertly tailored, and fit his slender but masculine frame perfectly. I detected the fragrance of Creed Aventus cologne.

"Detective Graham," he said. "Please sit." He reached across his desk and shook my hand. He had a good grip. I sat in one of the two visitor's chairs that faced him as he took his seat again.

"I understand you're heading the investigation into the . . ."

"Murders," I said.

"Chief Briggs tells me you're the best."

"The chief suffers from *favorite son syndrome*," I said.

He smiled and said, "I'm sure with such confidence we'll get to the bottom of this ugly business. What can I do to help?"

"We can start by telling me what you know."

"I've already told Detective McClusky all I know. What more can I tell you?"

"Everything you told Detective McClusky and anything more you might've recalled."

"It's all in McClusky's report," he said. "You just need to read it."

"I've read it," I said. "I'd like to hear it from you."

"You want to hear it again to compare my first interview," he said. "To see if I change anything. I know how you guys work."

"Guess I can't fool you," I said.

There was that reticence again. He was hesitant about how much he would give. For a man who had become entangled in a case involving multiple murders and was facing the potential demise of his business, it was reasonable to think he'd be more eager to help.

He said it had been a nightmare. "If it gets out of hand, the adverse publicity will destroy my business."

"From the number of times your reception room phone rang, I'm sure you have nothing to worry about just yet."

"The ladies are afraid to work," he said. "I've already had several tell me they won't take a client until this thing is over."

This guy seemed more concerned about saving his business than the murders of two innocent women. I was already getting a bad feeling about him. "You seem to have more concern for yourself than the two women who died," I said.

That took him by surprise. He did a one-eighty with his demeanor and said, "Detective Graham, I'm not a heartless man. I knew Marianne and Kim very well, professionally, of course. I attended both their funerals and didn't hold back my tears. But I've worked hard and long building my business, it's my whole life. I've never been married and I don't have children. Don't misconstrue my business concerns for callousness."

He seemed sincere, and I thought I might have been wrong in my judgment of him. But my cynicism told me to be careful. I said, "Just so we understand each other."

I had McClusky's report with me. I opened it on my lap and said, "Talk to me."

Benning leaned forward in his chair and laced his fingers together on his desk. As he talked, I referred to the report, following what Benning was saying and listening for any variation in his word choice or a change of inflection in his narrative. I let him talk without interruption. He was repeating what he had told McClusky, with minor variations. I had no reason not to believe he was telling the truth. But there was something about this guy that bothered me.

"Did the victims know each other?"

"All the ladies work free-lance," he said. "I supply an employee list to each of them with pertinent info about their fellow workers, but as far as socializing goes, I don't know how friendly they are with each other."

"But it's possible they might have been at least acquainted?"

"It's possible."

"And you can't say for sure the victims had any connection to each other, other than they were both employed by you?"

"I can't," he said.

"I'm sure you keep employee records."

"Only on their work ethics and behavior. I keep out of their personal lives."

"What's your vetting process?"

"I interview each employee. I don't keep a record of their interviews. If they measure up to my expectation, I hire them. Of course, I keep their personal info, name, age, present address, and emergency contacts. Otherwise, they are on their own."

"Do you solicit clients?"

"We have a small advertising account, but most of our clients are referrals. Potential clients phone in their requests and needs. I review the information concerning a client and, after checking their credentials, I assign an employee I believe would be most favorable to that client's needs. The employee decides if they're comfortable with the client, then set their own price and make their own deals. The company receives twenty percent of the revenue based on a minimum hourly rate. It's simple and efficient."

"What do you require from potential employees?"

"They're of legal age, unmarried, independent of alcohol and drugs, and they have no criminal record."

"And out of this world, beautiful," I said.

He smiled and said, "An obvious prerequisite."

"What about boyfriends?"

"Irrelevant as far as company rules go. As long as there is no conflict, I allow it."

"Do you accept women as clients?"

"Yes. As long as they meet our criteria. Of course, we have more male clients than females."

"And the ladies can refuse any client?"

"For whatever their reason. I don't question it."

"How can you be certain there are no improprieties?"

"By improprieties, you mean sexual favors?"

I nodded.

"Impropriety is a generic term," he said. "What people do behind closed doors is their business."

"Do you employ male escorts?"

"Not enough call for it."

"Do you maintain a record of past clients?"

"I'm required by law."

"I'll need those names going back twelve months."

"Not a problem."

He picked up his phone and spoke into it. In less than a minute, my new-found friend from the reception desk entered the room and handed me a sheet of paper. I said, "Thank you." She offered me a friendly smile and sashayed out the door.

I slipped the sheet of paper behind the report and scanned the report pages to see if McClusky had missed asking questions I would have asked.

I said, "Do you have an opinion about why these murders may have occurred?"

"I've been shredding my brain to find a plausible reason. The whole thing is bizarre."

"How did you arrive at the name *Moonlight Ladies* for your business?"

"It was my partner's wife who thought of it," he said. "We were searching for a suitable name when she suggested Moonlight Ladies, since most of the escorts are arranged for the evening or nighttime hours."

"Appropriate," I said.

"We thought so."

I closed the folder and stood up. "Thanks for your time," I said. "I'll keep you informed on a need-to-know basis."

He walked with me to the door and held it open. I paused before I left, sensing he had something more he wanted to say. In a low voice, he asked if there could be more murders.

I said, "Until we find a motive, bet on *yes*."

Chapter 3

Adrianna Blanchet was the first name on my list of current employees. She rented a suite in the Highgate Towers on Central Park West and had been employed by Moonlight Ladies since its beginning. The list in McClusky's file only supplied names and addresses and employment starting dates. If I wanted to know more, I'd have to find out for myself. To let the element of surprise work in my favor, I didn't call ahead for these interviews. A person who is off balance is less likely to lie.

I parked across from the Highgate Building, walked through the main lobby, and took an elevator up to the seventh floor. A poshly decorated corridor ran for what seemed like a quarter-mile before I arrived at Blanchett's apartment. A small speaker box in the doorframe included a door button. I pushed the button and waited. In an instant, a woman's voice called through the speaker box. "What can I do for you?"

"Detective Graham," I said, "with the New York City Police Department. I'm looking for Adrianna Blanchet."

"The voice said, "Is this about Moonlight Ladies?"

"It is," I said.

A security buzzer sounded, and the door lock was released electronically. I pushed the door open and stepped into a large, elaborately decorated living area, brightly lit by a set of floor-to-ceiling windows that offered a view of the New York City skyline. The décor was high-end. The air was heavy with perfume and stale cigarette smoke. A woman appeared across the room as I closed the door. Adrianna Blanchet was stunningly attractive. She appeared older than her thumbnail photo, but time had only aggrandized her beauty. Her blonde hair cascaded onto her shoulders and the highlights shimmered in the window light as she sauntered toward me. She was dressed in satin lounge wear and low-heeled bedroom slippers. She offered me a delicate hand and a friendly smile. I shook her hand and returned the smile.

"Thank you for seeing me," I said.

"This business is ugly and frightening," she said as she guided me to a plush sectional sofa where we sat. "How can I help?"

"I'm interviewing the current moonlight employees," I said. "I want to know what it is like to work for Mr. Benning."

Do you know who the monster is?

"I've just begun my investigation," I said.

"Do you have any *leans*?" she said.

"*Leads*," I said. "Tell me about Mr. Benning."

"Do you have any?"

"Any what?"

"Leads," she said.

"Only the one that brought me to you," I said.

She raised her eyebrows, and said, "Oh," then kicked off her slippers, tucked her legs under her, paused to collect her thoughts, and said, "I've been with Hayden—uh, Mr. Benning since he created the service. I was one of his first employees."

"How did you start working for him?"

"We dated in college. Nothing serious, just on and off. After graduation, we parted ways. I worked for several years in the corporate world; married, divorced, and soon found myself unemployed. I chose to leave my position seeking advancement in my chosen profession elsewhere. By a stroke of fate, I ran into Mr. Benning, who offered me a job in his newly formed agency. I accepted his offer and have never regretted it . . . until now." Then she added, "I'm so afraid."

"And you're happy with your employment and the way Mr. Benning treats you?"

"Mr. Benning has treated me with respect and caring. I'm sure he treats all his employees the same way. As long as we follow company rules, there's never a problem."

"Are you familiar with any of your other co-workers?"

"I wouldn't call them co-workers. We all freelance. Each of us has a relationship solely with Mr. Benning. There's little interaction between us. Unless Mr. Benning calls an employee meeting."

You know each other but don't get together often?

"I can't speak for the other girls, but I choose not to socialize much."

I took my list from my jacket pocket and handed it to her. "Do you know any names on this list?" I said.

She looked over the list and said, "I know the names, but I'd be hard-pressed to put a face to one. We don't see each other often. I am sure these girls are as scared as I am. I haven't worked in several weeks and told Hayden—uh, Mr. Benning, I have no intention of doing so until this nightmare is over. I mean, why would someone want to do this?"

I stood and slipped the list back into my pocket. "Can you think of a reason why someone would harm those women?"

"I couldn't fathom a reason."

I took my card from my pocket and handed it to her. "Thank you for your time," I said. "If you think of anything that might be useful, give me a call."

"I try not to think about it," she said.

I spent the rest of the afternoon interviewing the current employees on the list. My head was spinning by the amount of elegance and charm I'd seen in these women. Benning knew how to pick them. Adrianna Blanchet hadn't offered much other than her display of hero worship for Hayden Benning, which may have been contrived.

By three o'clock, I had interviewed four women. Each one told me the same basic story about their association with Moonlight Ladies and their relationship with Hayden Benning; every one of them regarded him as a good employer and a decent man.

It was past noon and my stomach was rumbling. I pulled into a Dunkin' and got a large black coffee and a croissant and sat at a table in the small dining area to take advantage of the air conditioning. While I ate, I scanned the list and noted the next name to be interviewed was Samantha Evers. She rented an apartment on 64th Street. I finished my lunch and headed in that direction.

Samantha Evers answered her door, wearing loose shorts and a gray sleeveless sweatshirt. I took her to be in her early twenties. She possessed a youthful beauty that exuded physical fitness. Her black hair was fashioned in short soft curls and her eyes were deep emerald green, both contrasted against the red sweatband stretched around her head. I couldn't help noticing the heart-shaped tattoo that sat in vibrant colors on the well-defined muscles of her upper arm; in a blue ribbon encircling the heart was the name **"Leon"** in bold letters. She was out of breath when she said, "I'm not interested."

When I showed her my shield, she said, "This is about the escort service, isn't it?"

I said, "Just a few questions."

I stepped into the coolness of an air-conditioned entranceway. She closed and bolted the door behind us, then led me to a large living area. The place was neat and modestly decorated, unlike the poshness I'd seen in the living quarters of the previous escort ladies. An overstuffed sofa sat in the center of the room between two mahogany end tables. Upon each table sat a five-pound dumbbell in a vertical position fashioned as a lamp. There was a piece of rectangular carpet beneath a treadmill, ostensibly to protect the polished hardwood floor. A large screen TV stood against one wall. A portable bar stood in one corner. There was a rack of free weights under the windows. The room felt like a gym rather than a Livingroom.

"I wondered how long it would be before the police questioned me," Samantha Evers said.

She stepped onto the treadmill, pushed the start button, and started a brisk walk while signaling me to have a seat on the sofa.

"Do you, mind?" she said. "I never break my training."

"As long as you can walk and talk," I said

"You mean like walk and chew gum?"

She smiled, never breaking the rhythm of her steps.

"I'm not in the habit of letting strange men into my apartment," she said. "But I couldn't resist your creamy brown eyes,"

I said, "My wife likes them too."

She looked only slightly disappointed.

I said, "What do you know about the murders?"

"Somebody killed two escorts for no reason."

"Someone had a reason," I said.

"This whole thing sucks," she said. "I haven't worked in weeks."

She stopped the treadmill, stepped off, took a deep breath, and let it out slowly. Then she read her pulse.

"One ninety-five," she said.

I said, "Is that good?"

"It is for me," she said on her way to the bar.

"Did you know the two victims?" I said.

"Not personally," she said.

I watched her fill two glasses with a hazy liquid and drop in some ice. She brought the glasses back to the sofa and handed me one. "Lemonade," she said. "I don't drink alcohol."

"Thanks," I said. I took a drink. It was cold enough to chatter my molars and sour enough to pucker my lips. When I could use my lips again, I said, "How long have you worked for the agency?"

"Just over two years," she said. She sat beside me on the sofa and sipped her drink as we spoke.

"How did you get the job?"

"I was fresh out of college and looking for a position in corporate marketing. It seemed, in every case, they expected me to assume a position to get a position. After I was tired of saying *thanks, but no thanks* to a bunch of carnal predators, my sister convinced me to accept an offer of employment from Mr. Benning.

"Your sister knows Mr. Benning?"

"She's been working for him for five years."

"In what capacity?"

"She's a moonlight lady escort."

I removed the employee list from my pocket and handed it to her. "Is your sister's name on this list?" I said.

She gave the list a once over and then handed it back to me. "Third from the top," she said. "Two names above mine."

The third name from the top was Adrianna Blanchet. I said, "Your sister is Adrianna Blanchet?"

"Yeah. She uses her married name, although she's been divorced for years."

Adrianna Blanchet had looked over the same list but never mentioned her sister. Why would she lie?

I didn't like being lied to.

I said, "Other than your sister, do you know any of the other ladies?"

"I know them by name, but rarely get together with any of them. I deal directly with Mr. Benning. He's a good man and treats me fairly."

I'd heard that laudation before. Either Benning was rapidly approaching sainthood or he had these women conned. My cynicism pushed my opinion toward the latter.

I handed her my card and said, “If you think of anything that might be helpful, call me.”

She brought the glasses back to the bar, then walked me to the door. When she reached up to unlatch the door, I noticed her tattoo again.

“Interesting tatt,”

“Thanks,” she said. “My boyfriend’s name in Leon. I surprised him with it last year.”

“Sort of like a brand,” I said.

She smiled.

People do strange things to themselves.

I said, “Thanks for your time.”

She said, “Come back and see me, brown eyes.”

CHAPTER 4

The next name on my list was Rosemarie Tuttle. She was living in a luxury condo on East 88th Street. I was close to that location, so I made it my last stop of the afternoon.

At the entrance to the 88th Street condos, a uniformed doorman approached me. He asked me what my business was. I told him I was there to see Rosemarie Tuttle. He said solicitors weren't allowed in the building.

I said, "I'm not selling," and showed him my shield.

"Is she in?" I said.

"She hasn't left the building all day."

"Is that usual for her?"

"She comes and goes when she pleases."

"You keep tabs on all the residents?"

"Just the hot-looking ones," he said.

He pointed to a bank of elevators at the far end of the lobby. I thanked him, chose an elevator, and pushed the green "up" button. When the doors opened, I stepped inside and said, "seven," to the elderly guy who was sitting on a stool pushing lighted numbered buttons. He was wearing a blue uniform with purple epaulets. A gold nametag that read "William Osterdash" was pinned to his lapel. He appeared to be in his eighties with sparse gray hair and loose doughy flesh. His face was clean-shaven but you couldn't tell from the roadmap of wrinkles that covered his cheeks and forehead. He pressed a button, and the elevator jerked into motion. We rode up for a couple of floors in silence, until he said, "Are you here for the convention?"

I said, "I'm here to see Miss Tuttle."

He said, "7-B."

I said, "Do you know her?"

"Everyone knows Miss Tuttle, he said. "She's good people."

I said, "Do you know all your riders?"

He smiled and said, "Just the hot-looking ones."

Age has no boundaries.

The elevator doors opened on the seventh floor. I thanked Osterdash and walked down a carpeted hallway and found Rosemarie Tuttle's apartment without issue. An issue arose when I noticed her apartment door ajar. It was quiet behind the door. I used my foot to push the door back a few inches and peered into a dimly lit hallway.

At the far end, I could see a large room. I called out, "Rosemarie Tuttle. NYPD."

Experience has taught me that when you find a door unlocked and opened and there is no answer from the other side. What you find on the other side is not good.

I slid my gun from its holster, released the safety, and pushed the door back the rest of the way. I walked through the hallway and into the room beyond. The subdued light coming from the windows facing the street broke the darkness. Between the light and shadow, I saw a neatly furnished room. The window light painted irregular rectangles on the carpeted floor. As I moved deeper into the room, I saw the figure of a woman lying on the carpet bathed in a silver rectangle of light. I knew she was dead. When you deal with death as much as I have, you know it without question. As I stepped closer, I recognized Rosemarie Tuttle from her thumbnail photo. Even in death, her beauty was evident. I kneeled beside her and felt her carotid artery. There was no pulse, no blood, or signs of physical abuse. Red bruising around her neck told me someone had strangled her. Her lifeless eyes stared into the darkness. I reached over and closed her eyelids.

After I'd called in the homicide. I went out to the hallway. There was a door at the end of the hall which opened to the stairs. Anyone wanting to leave the building could have taken the stairs down to the lobby and made their way to the street unnoticed.

I walked to the closest elevator and pushed the green button. The doors opened, revealing a young girl with a ponytail and thick glasses sitting on a stool. She wore the same uniform as Osterdash. When I held the doors open with my foot, she jumped off her stool and said, "What is this, mister? Let go of that door or I'll buzz security."

When I held up my shield, she said, "Why didn't you do that in the first place?"

I said, "Have you ridden anyone up or down from this floor this afternoon that you weren't familiar with? Someone that might have looked suspicious."

She thought for a moment, then said, "I don't think so. What are you after, mister?"

I said, "Where is Mr. Osterdash?"

"William operates car number four," she said. "This is number one." She leaned out and pointed down the hallway.

"You need to count three down from here," she said.

I removed my foot from the doors and said, "Thanks, I'll have to work on my numbers."

I walked down to the last elevator and pushed the blinking red button. I watched the numbers above the doors count down to the lobby, and then back up to floor seven. When the red button turned green, the doors opened. Osterdash was still sitting in his driver's seat. He said, "Leaving already? I'm sure Miss Tuttle is in. Would you like me to buzz her room?"

"Not necessary," I said. "I found her."

I got in and we started down.

I said, "How many people have you brought up to this floor today, William?"

He said, "Are you kidding?"

I said, "Try to remember."

He said, "Why do you want to know?"

When I showed him my shield, he said, "I guess, maybe, twenty-odd."

"Men and woman?"

"They're the only kind that rides," he said. "Animals aren't allowed in the building. Besides, they have trouble pushing buttons."

Witty for his age.

"Were there any ones you weren't familiar with? Strangers?"

"I pride myself on knowing my riders."

"Great. But I want to know about strangers."

He pursed his lips in thought and said, "I took a guy up around noon. He was wearing an expensive suit. And he smelled like an aristocrat—too much cologne."

"What did he look like?"

"About your height. I didn't notice his face. He was standing behind me."

"Did he say anything?"

"No. When we reached seven, he got out."

"Was there anything that stood out about him?"

"Just his expensive suit . . . and the way he smelled."

"Is there anyone else that sticks out in your mind?"

"Only that guy," he said, "because of his cologne." Then he scratched his head and said, "There was that woman with the pink dress and the big hat. I'd never seen her before. I remember her because of the hat."

"Guess you didn't see her face either."

"She had on sunglasses."

"She kept her sunglasses on in the elevator?"

He shrugged his shoulders.

"Young or old?"

"A young woman,"

"What color hair?"

"The hat covered it."

"Did she say anything?"

"She said, 'Nice day.' I said. 'It sure is.'"

"Did she say anything else?"

"No."

"What did she do then?"

"Got off at seven."

"Did you notice where she went?"

"No. I closed the doors and went down."

"Did you see her or the guy who wore too much cologne after that?"

"Not the guy. But I rode the woman down about twenty minutes later. You can check with Maggie in car number one. She's been here a long time and knows all the regulars."

"I already have," I said. "What about the other operators?"

"There are only two cars in service today."

"Did the woman say anything when you rode her down?"

"No. She got out at the lobby."

"Which way did she go?"

"Don't know. I closed the doors and went up."

When the elevator doors opened to the lobby, I slipped Osterdash a ten and left him with a smile on his face and his mind swirling with unanswered questions. I walked across the lobby to the front entrance, looking for the doorman I'd spoken with when I'd arrived. He was outside by the curb, hailing a cab. I waited until the cab took its fare and drove off. When he saw me, he said, "You're the cop. Did you find your lady?"

"I did," I said.

I followed him back to his post by the entrance and said, "Do you recall anyone entering the building today that you weren't familiar with?"

"People enter and leave the building all day: maintenance people, visiting relatives, couriers, doctors, lawyers—"

"I get it," I said. "I mean anyone that you remember who looked odd or suspicious."

"Everyone in this city looks odd to me," he said. "This is New York."

"What about the ladies? Did you see any hot looking ones today?"

"Just the one with the big hat," he said.

"What did she look like?"

"She had a nice—"

"I mean her face."

"I couldn't tell you. She wore sunglasses and that hat."

"Did she say anything?"

"Not a word. I watched her sashay across the lobby and take an elevator up."

"Have you seen her since?"

"A short time later, she came down. She hurried through the lobby and out the front door. "

"Did you see which way she went?"

"No."

I thanked him and went out to my car.

Someone whose motive for killing, known only to them, had murdered Rosemarie Tuttle. I'd never met Miss Tuttle, but I felt the sadness and wanton loss of the life of a beautiful young woman. No matter how many times I'd witnessed death, there had always been a disquieting of emotions—sadness and anger are the two that dominate my response.

Rosemarie Tuttle had been number *six* on my list of interviews, but number *four* on her killer's list of murders.

Chapter 5

Danny was sitting on the edge of my desk looking over the list of Moonlight Ladies' previous clients. I'd asked him to interview those he felt might be connected to the case.

"These murders aren't random," I said. "There's a connection somewhere. Four killings in almost as many months."

"A timetable of murders," Danny said. "Some on the list are from out of the country. Visiting dignitaries, business executives, and heads of state. The list is too extensive. We couldn't check everyone out."

"I didn't expect you to," I said.

"I concentrated on the ones that live in the metro area. All were successful business executives requiring an escort for whatever their needs were."

"And you came up with nothing?"

"I'm satisfied with all but one," Danny said. "George DeMarco. He lives in West Chester. He's the owner of a lumber mill that serves the northeast. A big-time company located with mills around the Metro area."

"What don't you like about him?"

"When I dug into his past. I found he'd been arrested several years ago for battery. His wife pressed charges against him. The charges were dropped, and they divorced, but from the statement she gave police, she was lucky to leave the marriage in one piece."

"Nice guy," I said.

"That's not all," Danny said. "Last year, he was arrested for A and B on his live-In girlfriend. He plea-bargained it out. Paid the fine and walked."

"This guy's got problems," I said.

"And good connections," Danny said.

"Yeah, money can do that. When was the last time he used the escort service?"

Danny referred to his list. "Eight months ago. Victoria Quinlan accompanied him to a northeast lumber convention. It's a two hundred dollar a plate annual dinner, speeches, awards, and business meetings all took place right here in the city at the Waldorf. She'd accompanied him twice before that to different venues."

"Where does Miss Quinlan live?"

Danny checked his sheet and said, "Prospect Heights."

"Continue with your list," I said. "Find out what you can. I'll visit Quinlan and see what else she can tell us about this guy. It's a long shot, but worth the effort."

"No stone left unturned," Danny said.

"You're learning," I said

***

I arrived at Park Place in Prospect Heights and found a parking space across the street from Victoria Quinlan's residence. The neighborhood was high-end. Rows of well-kept brownstones lined both sides of the street. I climbed the stone steps to the front door and rang the bell. A young woman opened the door, wearing a flowered shirt and white Capri pants. Her red hair was cut short and her blue eyes sparkled in the sunlight.

Before I could ID myself, she said, "I'm not interested."

I showed her my shield and said, "I'm looking for Victoria Quinlan."

"I wondered how long it would take the police to question me," she said.

She opened the door wider, and I followed her through a short vestibule into a large living room. She sat on the sofa. I sat in an armchair opposite her.

"What do you know about the murders?" I said.

"Three escorts were killed for no reason," she said.

"Someone had a reason," I said.

"Of course," she said. "What do you want to know?"

"Whatever you can tell me about one of your past clients, George DeMarco."

"Is he a suspect ?" she said.

"A person of interest."

I could see the consternation on her face when she heard DeMarco's name. She was thinking about what she wanted to say and how she wanted to say it.

"I supplied an escort for Mr. DeMarco more than once," she said.

"Three, in six months," I said.

"You've done your homework.

"I wasn't good in the classroom," I said. "But I was good at homework."

She smiled and continued. "DeMarco is rich, owns a lumber company in—"

"I'm familiar with Mr. DeMarco's background," I said. "I'd like your assessment of him."

"You mean what he's like?"

"Whatever you can tell me."

"He was what you'd expect from a millionaire CEO. They all come from the same mold. We got along fine until our second encounter."

I let her continue.

"He began to get too familiar with me. That's not the way escorts work. It's all business. I've never had a problem with any client before."

"He made advances toward you?"

"Not sexually. He expected more from me. He became more demanding, too familiar, less respectful, too aggressive."

"Aggressive how?"

"He got too hands-on. If he wanted me to walk with him, he'd pull me along by my arm. After a while, I felt he believed women were subservient to a man of his stature."

"Familiarity breeds contempt," I said. "Did he ever abuse you?"

"Hit me?"

"Yes."

"No, but sometimes I thought he might. When he raised his voice to me in anger. In time, I became uncomfortable in his presence, almost afraid to be with him. It wasn't long before I'd had enough. I had to refuse him as a client."

"Was Mr. Benning aware of this?"

"Yes. After I told Mr. Benning how I felt, he informed Mr. DeMarco his future requests would be denied. Mr. Benning dropped him from his client list."

"How did DeMarco take your rejection of him?"

"He phoned me the following day and tried to make amends. When I refused his gestures, he became belligerent. I sensed the threats in his voice. He said I'd be sorry for making him look like a fool."

"Sorry, how?"

"I didn't ask."

When I stood, she stood with me. "Have you heard from him since?" I said.

"No, but sometimes I feel I'm being watched. An experience like that is something you don't shake off easily."

I handed her my card and said, "If you hear from him, or you remember something you want to tell me. Please give me a call."

She said, "I'm sure I won't hear from him again. But thanks, I will."

I said thanks and left.

Back at headquarters, I scanned over the lists of clients, employees, and victims, trying to put the pieces of the puzzle together. Between the interviews, I had taken and the work Danny had done with his list; we had gathered an abundance of information concerning the Moonlight Ladies' daily operation, but nothing definitive that would connect any of the players to the murders. The information Victoria Quinlan had given me about George DeMarco told me he was a man of an intemperate personality, but that didn't make him a murderer. A check of the client list revealed that the three times he had used the agency had been with Victoria Quinlan as his escort. I'd keep him on my list and check him out further if the situation warranted it.

I was about to grab some lunch when I received a call from Hayden Benning. He sounded distressed. "I received a letter—a note in a plan unaddressed envelope," he said. "Somebody slipped it under the door of the outer office. I found it when I arrived this morning."

"What kind of note?"

"A ransom demand."

"Ransom for what?"

"A monetary payment to make the killings stop."

I said, "I'll be right over."

I made it to Fifth Avenue in good time. The front office of Moonlight Ladies was empty, except for Ashley Allan, behind the reception desk. She looked up from her computer screen when she saw me and followed me with her eyes. As I walked past her toward Benning's office, she pointed a finger at me with a smile and said, "Graham, like the crackers. I just got it." I smiled and gave her a thumbs up, then opened the door to Benning's office and went in.

As I entered, Benning was at his desk, pouring himself a drink from a cut-glass decanter. He downed the drink, took a deep breath, and slid the decanter toward me. I shook my head.

He was dressed in a three-piece suit and looked as handsome and squeaky clean as he had been. Despite his outward appearance, the anxiety in his eyes was apparent.

He pointed to a legal size manila envelope on his desk. I picked it up from a corner and removed a single sheet of paper. The paper was colored blue, which I found unusual and interesting. I unfolded it by its edges and read the block letters that were written in black marker. The simple message demanded a fifty-thousand dollar payment for a guarantee that the killings would stop. There were no particulars about how to deliver the money, just a simple note at the bottom stating there would be further instructions.

"Other than yourself, and the deliverer, has anyone else handled this envelope or its contents?"

"No. I was the first one to arrive this morning when I found it."

He poured himself another drink and threw it down. "What should I do? I don't have fifty thousand dollars to give away. But if these killings continue, I won't have a business much longer."

I said, "Try easing up on that hooch first. It won't help you make rational decisions."

He put the stopper in the decanter and put it and the glass in the side drawer of his desk. "I'm unable to accommodate clients," he said. "The ladies are too afraid to work. A situation like that is unsustainable. And now a ransom demand. What do you suggest I do, detective?"

"Until we get further instruction, there's nothing we can do," I said. "I'll give this to the crime lab, and see if we can identify its author. Until you hear from me or receive further instructions, do nothing."

"Do you expect me to sit here and twiddle my thumbs and watch my business get destroyed?" he said.

"Maybe you should contact your employees and reassure them that everything is being done. It might ease their concerns."

Benning was, again, thinking more about his business than the welfare of his employees. His attitude was annoying me.

I put the note back into the envelope and slid it into the inside pocket of my jacket.

"I'll be in touch," I said. Then I left Benning to twiddle his thumbs.

CHAPTER 6

When I got back to my desk, I received a call from the assistant medical examiner, Doctor Laurie Geffkin. She identified herself as having been the surgeon who performed the autopsies on all three of the Moonlight ladies' victims. She said she had something of significance; she thought I should see it firsthand.

The Chief Medical Examiner's Office is on E. 26th Street in Manhattan. I took an elevator to the third floor office of Dr. Geffkin. There was no one in the office, so I knocked on the door again and called out my name. A woman stepped out of an inner office door. She had short black hair, fashionably kept, and was wearing a white lab coat, heels, and black slacks. "Detective Graham," she said. "I'm sorry I didn't hear. My person isn't back from lunch yet."

She closed the door behind her and said, "Let's go to the morgue. You'll want to see what I have to show you."

We rode an elevator to the basement. I followed her down a hygienic hallway of white-glazed tiles. I smelled death in the air. When you deal with death every day, you know its presence. We pushed through a pair of stainless steel double doors and walked into a large autopsy theater. At a wall of freezer cabinets, Geffkin pulled open a drawer in the center of the bottom row. "Although the facts are in my report," she said. "I thought you'd want to see for yourself something that could be overlooked."

She folded the sheet back, revealing the head, neck, and shoulders of a young woman. "The moonlight murderer's fourth victim," she said.

Even in death, I recognized the lovely face of Rosemarie Tuttle. Against her pallid skin, I could see bruising around her neck.

"My official cause of death is asphyxiation from strangulation, consistent with the prior two victims. "

I leaned forward for a closer look. "What are those marks on the front of her neck?" I said.

"That's what I wanted to show you."

"They look like punctures."

"They're not punctures," she said. "The skin wasn't broken."

"Then what are they?"

"Indentations."

"Made by what?"

"Someone with long fingernails."

When she offered no further explanation, I said, "A woman?"

She said, "Someone with long fingernails."

"Did you find the same indentations on the other victims?"

"Yes. They were almost identical in each case."

"So, whoever strangled these women had fingernails long enough to make those marks?"

"Without question," she said. "The pattern reveals the killer came up from behind his victim, which allows the use of four fingers on each hand to apply pressure to the trachea and cut off the air supply. If strangulation took place from the front, the thumbs would be the only source to apply pressure. There is more strength in four fingers than in two thumbs. Death would occur more quickly."

"So the victims were all taken by surprise from behind?"

"That's what the markings tell me."

"Is this an official finding or your opinion?" I said.

"My opinion, based on the physical evidence and fifteen years of examining bodies. It's in my report."

"You can't tell if the markings are from a man or woman?"

Geffkin shook her head. "Too bad we can't identify fingernails like we do fingerprints," she said. "If we could, you'd have your killer."

Every woman I had questioned on my list had fingernails manicured and polished. It was easy to spot that much care and detail. My guess was any of those nails were long enough to leave the indentations I'd seen on Rosemarie Tuttle's neck.

I thanked Doctor Geffkin and headed back to headquarters.

Danny was waiting for me at my desk. "The rest of the list is cold," he said. "I see nothing significant to tie any of the former clients to the case."

I trusted Danny's good judgment and eliminated the list and the clients on it from any further investigation. I had dropped off Hayden Benning's ransom note at forensics for a full examination. I'd wait and see if they pull anything from it. In the meantime, I wanted to talk with George DeMarco.

DeMarco kept a mobile office in a lumber yard in South Jersey. Danny and I made the hour drive and arrived unannounced. His office was in a low flat roof building that sat on a couple of acres of land. I maneuvered the Chevy through a gravel road, passing piles of felled trees and bundles of cut lumber. There was a gravel parking lot beside the building. I parked between two pickups and cut the engine.

Danny said, "How do you want to handle this?"

"Let's see what this guy's all about," I said. "I expect him to deny everything Victoria Quinlan claimed about him."

We got out and walked toward the office. After Danny gave the door a couple of knuckle wraps, the door opened about eight inches and a red faced, beady eyed guy looked out at us with an unfriendly face. He said, "Yeah?"

I showed him my shield. "We're here to see Mr. DeMarco," I said.

He looked at my shield, then said, "Ya got papers?"

I said, "Papers for what?"

He said, "I know plenty of places can make up a badge like that."

I looked at Danny.

Danny looked at me.

Was this guy kidding?

I took a business card out of my wallet and showed it to him. He squinted his beady eyes as he looked it over, then opened the door the rest of the way. This guy was built like a lumberjack, thick and wide across the shoulders and at least six-four. The sleeves of his red flannel shirt strangled his huge biceps. He looked like a bully, too dumb to be afraid of anyone or anything.

We stepped into a small, disorderly office. A window air conditioning unit was blasting cold air across the small room, aimed at DeMarco, who was sitting behind a desk talking on a cellphone. When we entered, he didn't look at us.

I guessed DeMarco to be about forty. He carried a good tan and his black hair was cropped close to his head. There must have been a sale on red flannel shirts at the *Clothes Mart.* DeMarco wore his with the sleeves rolled up to his elbows, and the collar opened. When he finished his conversation, he tossed the phone onto his desk and said. "Idiots think we grow trees," As he looked up at us, lumberjack said. "Police officers."

I held up my shield and said, "Detectives Graham and Nolan, NYPD."

Lumberjack looked at DeMarco and said, "Okay?"

DeMarco nodded, and the big guy disappeared into another room.

"What do you guys want?" DeMarco said.

Danny said, "Your name came up during our murder investigation. We'd like to ask you a few questions. Maybe you can help us out."

"Murder," DeMarco said. "What do I know about a murder?"

"Maybe nothing," I said. "If you give us the right answers."

DeMarco selected a cigar from a wooden box on his desk, then turned the box around to us. "Montecristo's," he said. "I know a guy."

I knew Montecristo's were expensive Cuban cigars, not the kind a guy earning less than six figures could indulge.

When we declined his offer, DeMarco slapped the lid closed and said, "This is about the Moonlight Ladies, ain't it? I read about it. They're saying it's a serial killer."

I watched him remove the cellophane from the cigar and place it in an ashtray on his desk. He slid the cigar under his nostrils and gave it a quick sniff. Then he cut the tip with a guillotine cutter and placed the clipping in the ashtray. He rolled the cut end of the cigar between his lips, wetting it to his satisfaction. The degree of attention he gave to the process was ceremonious. He executed each step with meticulous precision and an equal degree of concentration. The esteem he held for a piece of rolled tobacco was inordinate.

He removed a chrome lighter from his shirt pocket and touched the flame to the cigar end, rotating the end to assure an even light. He drew on the cigar and let the smoke out easily, savoring every moment with orgasmic pleasure. Then he leaned back in his chair and said, "Okay. What do you wanna know?"

"Your relationship with Victoria Quinlan," I said.

"What relationship?" he said. "I rented her through Moonlight Ladies a couple of times."

"When I interviewed her, she said she had a problem with you," I said. "Said you threatened her after Benning removed you from the escort list because she voiced her dissatisfaction with your behavior."

"She's a liar," he said. "She's pissed off because I didn't tip her. I don't tip. Benning gets enough money for his girls. She's an airhead bimbo. Thinks she's better than everyone else because she wears pearls and fancy dresses and works for Hayden Benning. I know how to handle that type."

"How well do you know Hayden Benning?" Danny said.

"Met him once. I went to his office to let him know how pissed I was at being disrespected like I was. He was more self-absorbed in himself and his business than in his treatment of the women that work for him. Quinlan said she thought he was a tyrant."

"She spoke well of Benning when I interviewed her," I said.

"Probably afraid to tell the truth to a cop. She told me Benning treated all his girls badly. Gave them no say in who they escorted and set strict rules for them to follow. She said she hated him. Her loose lips catch up with her loose brain when she has a few drinks."

"Why do the girls stay with him?" Danny said.

"He pays well."

"Then you deny any friction between you and Miss. Quinlan?" I said.

"If you want to call it friction," he said. "When she didn't behave, I had to put her in her place."

"Put her in her place?" I said.

"Sure. I paid good money for her. I expect to get what I pay for."

Danny said. "If you weren't satisfied with her, why did you keep requesting her?"

"She's got nice tits. And she looked good on my arm."

"So you regarded her as more of an ornament than a companion," I said.

"I expect what I pay for. Sometimes women get big heads. You have to keep them under control."

"How'd you accomplish this control?" Danny said.

"I never laid a hand on her, if that's what you're getting at. And I sure as hell didn't murder her."

"No one said she'd been murdered?" Danny said.

"I—I thought since you were asking about her."

"She's alive and well," I said.

I removed a victim list from my pocket and handed it to him. "I can't say the same for these women," I said. "Have any of them ever escorted you?"

He said, "I don't know these women." Victoria Quinlan was the only one I rented."

When he handed me back the list, I dropped my business card on his desk and asked him to call if he remembered anything helpful. As we started for the door, DeMarco stood up and said, "I'd keep my eye on Benning if I were you. He's not what he pretends to be."

"Guess you believed Miss. Quinlan when she said he was a tyrant," Danny said.

"I know one when I see one," he said.

Back at the Chevy, Danny said, "Do you believe Quinlan or DeMarco?"

I said, "Quinlan. The misogyny was dripping off that guy."

"Yeah, like a bad sweat," Danny said.

"Doesn't make him a murderer," I said.

Danny said, ". . . Maybe."

CHAPTER 7

Sandy and I were enjoying lunch at Branigan's restaurant on 54th Street. It was our favorite place to eat. The elder Branigan had purchased the place back in the forties and ran it as a local watering hole. After his passing, his son Pete inherited the place and turned it into a full-fledged eatery. It offered a theme of historic Americana and catered to a diversity of people of all age groups, from college students to the elderly. Sandy and I felt comfortable somewhere in the middle. The perimeter walls were covered with Knotty-pine and varnished to a soft gloss, upon which hung framed posters of historic U.S. headlines from magazine covers and newspapers that had long since ceased publication. The dining room comprised round tables covered with white linen table clothes and a formal setting. A single faux rose in a clear plastic vase sat at the center of each table to add elegance to an otherwise rustic motif. For the more discreet, rows of dimly lit booths at the perimeter were available. A well-kept mahogany bar with a brass footrail and brass stools with red vinyl seat covers ran along the entire length of one wall. The kitchen served lunch and dinner seven days a week, touting the best clam chowder in Manhattan.

We had taken a booth by a front window that looked out onto the hustle and bustle that was New York City. I'd ordered a "house burger" with a side of fries. Sandy was working on a tuna sub. We shared a Caesar salad. I drank beer. She sipped a chardonnay over ice.

Sandra Sullivan was a Connecticut girl. Her father held the title of a county judge while her mother enjoyed the title of "wealthy homemaker." As an only child, she conceded her parents had pampered her until her father's death caused a falling out between her mother and her over the distribution of her father's estate. Things soured so badly that she was glad when she was accepted into Harvard and could move away from home.

I'd met Sandy during the several court appearances we'd shared over the years. As a defense attorney, she had grilled me to toast more than once on the witness stand. Our first casual conversation over lunch had been more antagonistic than friendly. She said she was a firm believer in civil obedience, which is why she practiced law. I told her that her belief system stemmed from her Irish catholic upbringing and I saw society and the law in a more realistic, cynical way. She said I had a lot to learn about human kindness. I told her I had seen little of that in my profession.

I often wondered how a girl like Sandy could hook up with an "average joe" like me. Some men might be wary of a woman like Sandy, threatened by her good looks, intelligence, and independents; but it was those very attributes that attracted me to her. That and the inexplicable good feeling I got whenever we were together. Call it love. Call it compatibility. I only knew our relationship "clicked" and I was playing my cards right. I didn't want to screw it up.

"A person needs their fingernails to be long to receive a proper manicure," Sandy said. "Men get manicures too."

"But more women do than men," I said.

She said, "Good thinking, detective."

"These murders are more likely to have been committed by a woman than a man," I said.

"But not necessarily," she said.

I said, "Good thinking, counselor."

"The fingernail evidence doesn't help you much," she said.

I refilled my glass from the pitcher on the table and topped off Sandy's glass from the chardonnay bottle. "Doesn't narrow it down either. Everyone has fingernails," I said.

"Once you establish motive, you'll be able to work from there."

"Right now I have nothing. The contrary views of Hayden Benning I got from Miss Quinlan and DeMarco don't amount to much more than their opinions."

"You said Adrianna Blanchet lied to you," Sandy said. "There's suspicion in that."

"There is," I said.

"Could she have missed her sister's name on the list?"

"She knew her sister worked for Benning. She should have told me."

Sandy said, "Not saying anything can also be a lie."

I drove Sandy back to the courthouse for her one-thirty court time and went back to headquarters. At my desk, I found a complete analysis report on my laptop screen from our forensics lab concerning the ransom note Hayden Benning had received.

The paper used was of common stock and the lettering was applied with black water based marker ink. No prints were found, nor any common trace elements. At the bottom of the page, a significant discovery was noted in bold letters. A chemical compound identified as "aldehyde" was found embedded in the paper fiber. The report stated the chemical was used in perfumery. I wanted to learn more about it, so I punched up the number for the forensics lab. The phone was answered quickly, but they asked me to hold. After almost ten minutes, a technician named Hurley picked up. I identified myself a second time and asked for a clearer explanation concerning the chemical found.

Hurley said, "Aldehyde is a chemical compound used to make fragrances. It had been absorbed into the paper fiber of the ransom note."

I said, “I didn’t smell any fragrance on it.”

“The fragrance weakens with time,” Hurley said, “to where it is undetectable.”

“How would it get absorbed into the paper?” I said.

“Several ways are possible,” he said. “My guess would be whoever wrote that note had applied a fragrance to himself or herself and the compound was still on the skin of their hands when they wrote the note. When they handled the paper, traces of it would have transferred into the fibers.”

“So, this chemical is used in men’s colognes and women’s perfumes?”

“Yes. Any topical application that releases a pleasant fragrance.”

I thanked Hurley and ended the call. I recalled detecting a floral fragrance of perfume from every woman I had interviewed on my list. Collectively, the fragrances were familiar, yet distinctly different.

I scanned the report on my screen again, looking for something more I could use to further my case. There was nothing but that enigmatic chemical.

Chapter 8

Ruth Ellison looked at me with pleading eyes. "I know my husband was murdered," she said.

"Why do you think so?" I said.

"Because I know my husband."

I had taken her call earlier that afternoon. She said she'd read in the papers I was leading the investigation into the Moonlight murders and she had information she knows would interest me. I told her I could see her anytime that afternoon. She showed up at my desk an hour later. She was sitting in my visitor's chair, wringing a handkerchief in her hands, looking uneasy. I took her to be in her mid-forties, modestly attractive with blond shoulder-length hair and fair skin. Although she was doing a courageous job of hiding her emotions, her face bore signs of stress. I saw uncertainty, sadness, and loneliness behind her eyes.

I recalled Mike Ellison had been Hayden Benning's business partner, who had taken his own life three years ago. Her claim someone had murdered her husband was questionable. I had read the investigator's report and found nothing to the contrary that Mike Ellison had killed himself. Yet, his widow was sitting in front of me, telling me she was sure someone had murdered him.

"The investigation into your husband's death concluded it was a suicide," I said. "Why would you believe otherwise?"

"Because of the Moonlight Ladies' murders," she said.

"You think there's a connection between your husband's death and the murders?"

"I've been living with a suspicion for three years," she said. "When these murders began, I felt more confident my suspicion was valid. Mike was indeed suffering from mental issues, but he had no intention of taking his own life. He had good reasons to live. We were happily married and planning a family. And Mike was looking forward to the business flourishing."

"Is there anyone who would benefit from your husband's death?"

"Mike had a life insurance policy naming me the beneficiary. I received a substantial amount that keeps me comfortable. As far as I know, he had no enemies."

"What about family?"

"Mike was an only child. His parents are both deceased."

"Why have you waited until now to bring this to someone's attention?"

She leaned closer to me as if to be sure I understood every word she said. "Who could I turn to?" she said. "When I read you were heading the moonlight investigation, I thought I'd found someone who might, at least, listen to me. I may not have the proof, but I know in my heart Mike was murdered."

"Based on what you've told me, why would someone want to kill your husband?"

"I don't know," she said. "I only know he didn't kill himself."

"You can't bring charges based on your intuition," I said. "You'll need proof."

"I've come to you hoping you'll help me find that proof." There was an urgent plea in her voice.

"What do you want me to do?"

"Look into the possibility that my husband was murdered," she said.

"You're asking me to re-investigate a case that has been closed for three years without a viable reason? If you have concrete evidence, your husband was murdered, it would be best if you told me about it."

"I know it sounds crazy," she said, "but I'm sure Mike didn't take his own life. Call it a wife's intuition. Call it whatever you want. I'm asking for your help. I can't continue with the uncertainty. Whether the evidence finds me right or wrong, at least I'll have closure."

I felt her anguish, but I wasn't comfortable with what she was asking me to do. However, my philosophy of leaving "no stone unturned" kicked in, and I knew I would look into her claim. If the moonlight ladies' killings were tied to her husband's death, I wanted to know how.

"I won't make any promises," I said. "But I'll look over the reports again to be sure nothing was overlooked. I'll keep you informed on a need to know basis."

She appeared satisfied by my offer. Her face brightened as if I had removed some of the weight she'd been carrying. She seemed like an honorable, decent woman, and I hoped in some small way I could help her. She thanked me with a handshake and left the bureau, feeling better than she had when she arrived.

I pulled up the Kings County medical examiner's report and read it a second time. It stated Mike Ellison had hung himself in his garage by tying a polypropylene rope around a ceiling beam and inserting his head into a noose at the other end. He had kicked out a folding chair from beneath his feet, therefore, dangling to his death. He didn't leave a suicide note, and they had found no evidence of foul play. The case had been closed without question. The report deemed the death a suicide, corroborating their police investigation. There were no signs of a struggle on the body, only bruising around the neck from the rope, and the crushing of the Hyoid bone in the throat, which is consistent with all strangulations.

I went a step further and phoned the 68th precinct in Brooklyn and spoke with Detective Martin Reynolds, who had led the investigation into the death of Mike Ellison. Reynolds told me he believed Ellison's death was a suicide and found nothing to the contrary.

I said, "Your report stated Ellison was found lying on his garage floor alongside a folding chair that had been turned on its side. How do you explain that?"

"It was determined Ellison hadn't secured the rope to the beam very well," Reynolds said. "After he hung there for a while, the knot slipped, causing the rope to slide off the beam and the body to fall to the floor."

"Is there evidence supporting that?"

"Just a theory," he said.

I supposed it wasn't an impossibility, but it seemed far-fetched since Ellison had served in the Navy and would have been proficient in the making of knots. I'm sure he would have chosen the appropriate knot for the job.

"Were there prints or DNA on the rope?"

"If there were, we couldn't pull them."

"Were there any other prints found?"

"None," he said.

"What about the chair?" I said. "It should have had Ellison's prints on them."

There was a short pause, then Reynolds said, "That's how the report reads."

"Is the rope available for inspection?"

"It should still be in our evidence room."

"Can you send me a photo of it?" I said. "A shot of its entire length and a closeup of both ends."

Reynolds said, "I'll get it to you asap."

I thanked Reynolds and ended the call.

CHAPTER 9

Chief Briggs called Danny and me into his office, looking for an update on our progress. He'd been getting his balls busted by the mayor and the city council about the moonlight murders. The press were continuing to publish stories about a possible serial killer in the city. The speculative journalism was upsetting the city council, and they took their frustration out on the police commissioner, who in turn laid his gloves on Chief Briggs.

So far, Briggs hadn't busted our balls. But mud rolls downhill and if we didn't come up with something tangible soon, he would have to put the heat on us.

Briggs read over our interim report as he spoke. "Is this DeMarco guy out of the picture?" he said.

"Not yet," I said. "He's got a violent past, a bad temper, and a perverse attitude toward women, but we've yet to find a motive for murder."

"And no criminal record," he said.

"Charges dropped or plea bargained out," I said.

"How's he hooked up with the agency?"

Danny said, "He's hired escorts in the past. He's had a problem with one girl and a heated argument with Hayden Benning. The details are in our report."

"Then he's a person of interest?" Briggs said.

"As of now," I said.

Briggs turned a page and said, "What have you gotten out of the ransom letter?"

"Forensics found nothing other than the presence of a chemical used to manufacture perfume embedded in the paper fibers.

"Written by a woman, then."

"Not necessarily," I said. "The chemical is also used in men's aftershave and colognes."

Briggs was getting annoyed because he wasn't getting the answers he'd hoped for from his line of questioning.

"What about former and current employees?"

"All vetted and interviewed," I said.

"Except for those that have left the country or we couldn't locate," Danny said.

"I wouldn't concern myself with those," Briggs said.

"We're not," I said.

"And you haven't come up with anything substantial yet?" Briggs said.

I looked at Danny. Danny looked at me. I said, "Not yet."

"I'll assign you some help," Briggs said.

"We don't need it," I said.

"Well, you haven't shown me much. I've got to tell the Mayor something."

"Tell him to sit on his hands," I said.

Briggs scowled.

Danny rescued me with, "We have several leads we're following. We'll have something for you by the weekend."

I hoped Danny knew something I didn't because I had nothing more to say to Briggs, except, "See you in the morning."

Back at my desk, I said to Danny, "What've you got to show the chief by the end of the week?"

He said, "Nothing. But I'm sure something'll come up."

As Danny walked back to his desk, I said, "Something better come up, or it's our ass."

Before I could say another word, my desk phone rang. I answered it with my usual, "Homicide, Detective Graham."

A quiet voice said, "This is Ashley Allan."

"Do I know you, Miss Allan?"

"I'm the secretary for Mr. Benning. You know, 'Graham like the crackers'."

"Oh, sure," I said. "What can I do for you."

"I came upon information I think you should know."

"About the case?"

"Yes. Can we speak privately?"

"I'll be at my desk in the morning," I said.

"I wouldn't want to wait till then. Can we talk this afternoon?"

"I'm just leaving for the day if—"

"I'm on 42nd Street," she said. "The Caledon building, apartment. 6a. If you come now, I can tell you everything."

There was no reason I couldn't accommodate her. Getting home to my apartment later than usual would be no big deal. I was to meet Sandy there by seven. We had planned to share a home-cooked dinner, a night of lovemaking, and a lineup of classic movies—not necessarily in that order.

I told Ashley Allan I'd see her in twenty minutes and ended the call.

***

When I met Ashley Allen at her apartment, she was wearing faded jeans and a worn sweatshirt. The antitheses of what I'd expected her to look like after having seen her at her reception desk. She wore no makeup. She didn't need it. Distress was evident on her face as she thanked me for coming and led me into a living area. The room had been furnished with a single sofa, a coffee table, and one faux leather armchair. A small desk sat in one corner, upon which sat a laptop and a cellphone cradle. A large screen TV and a stereo system were the only creature comforts visible. I had expected to find the same fashionable motif I had seen at the other moonlight lady's apartments. But, instead, found a comfortable, homey ambiance.

Ashley Allan sat on the sofa beside me and thought for a moment before she spoke. "I'm not sure where to begin," she said. "I've stumbled upon something I know is not right, and I struggled with myself before deciding to phone you."

"Take your time," I said, "and tell me what you think I should know."

"Yesterday evening, I was getting ready to leave work when I realized I'd forgotten to give Mr. Benning a client contract he'd been waiting for. He was still in his office, so I decided to leave it with him before I left. His office door was ajar and as I approached. I heard him in conversation on his phone. At first, the conversation sounded routine, but before I opened the door, I heard him say, "'You're in this as much as I am." She covered her mouth with her hand as if she'd regretted saying as much. I put a comforting hand on her shoulder and said, "You're doing fine."

She said, "I stepped back from the door while he continued the rest of his conversation. That's when I heard him say, "'If I go down for this, you'll go down with me.'"

I said, "What time did this happen?"

"A little past five. I know because I checked the time on my computer screen."

"Did you hear anything more?"

"I'd heard enough," she said. "I left the contract on my desk and went home. What do you think was the meaning of what he said?"

"Sometimes we can misinterpret a conversation and get it twisted up in our heads, causing undue worry." I gave her my card and told her to call my cell if she had more information or if she wanted to talk.

"I'm not comfortable going back to work," she said. "Do you think Mr. Benning has done something criminal?"

"We'll check it out. Meanwhile, don't show anguish or fear in his presence. I'm sure you're in no danger."

I took her hand and gave it a gentle squeeze. "You did the right thing by telling me this," I said. "It took guts."

She walked me to the door and thanked me for my support and understanding. "I'll trace the call and find out who Mr. Benning was talking to. If there's something you should know, I'll tell you."

I looked up Benning's business number, then called communications from my cell during my ride home. I asked them to search Benning's call activities on the day and time Ashley Allan had given me.

By the time I arrived at my apartment, I had what I needed. I sat in the Chevy and read the email communications sent to my cellphone. Benning had been talking to Andriana Blanchet at the time Ashley Allen overheard his conversation. The phone record also showed Benning had been making calls to Blanchet regularly. There were no calls to other escort ladies. Since Blanchet was Benning's employee, the phone call wasn't out of the ordinary. But what Ashley Allan had overheard was questionable. Benning's line: "If I go down for this, you'll go down with me," suggested wrongdoing. But there could be many explanations for it. Benning might be doing more than twiddling his thumbs.

Chapter 10

They were sitting at the kitchen table drinking shots of whiskey. He had downed one and made it a point to be sure Ellison had drained his glass twice. He reached across the table and poured him another.

"Whoa. Any more of these and Ruth will have my head when she gets home."

"You can handle a lot more than this," he said.

Ellison smiled and drained his glass again. His eyes were heavy. It was difficult to focus on the opened journal on the table before him. He ran his hand across the lined paper to stop the numbers from dancing across the page.

"What did you want to talk about?" he said. "On the phone, you said it was important."

"Let's have one more," he said, "before we talk details."

He filled both glasses again, then got up and walked to the front room window. He looked out at the car parked across the street. She was sitting in the driver's seat, waiting for him as he had instructed her to do. When he turned, Ellison was standing behind him. "What are you looking at?" Ellison said.

"It looks like snow," he said. "Let's sit by the fire. Our business can wait."

They sat in the armchairs by the hearth. The warmth of the fire was working on Ellison. His eyes became heavy and his head became light. It wasn't long before his head dropped against the chair's back.

Things were working out just as he'd planned. After today, his money worries would be over. He waited a full minute, then another minute until he heard heavy breathing. Then he got up and walked behind the armchair. He put his hands on Ellison's shoulders. They were rock hard. Age hadn't taken away the fitness of an ex-sailor.

Do it now, he told himself. Before you lose your courage.

He wrapped his fingers around Ellison's neck and squeezed. Ellison's body convulsed once, jolting him out of his stupor. He brought his hands up and tried to pry the sweaty finger from his throat, kicking his legs out and contorting his body. He couldn't shout. He couldn't scream. He couldn't breathe. The pressure increased. The room became a vortex of dark and light until Ellison's body went limp and his chin dropped to his chest.

He waited.

There was no breathing and no movement. Satisfied, he walked back to the window and signaled for her to come inside. She draped the coil of rope over her shoulder so she could carry the folding chair with both hands.

"Did you do it?" she said.

He pointed to Ellison, still and lifeless in the chair. The presence of the dead man sent a sick feeling throughout her body. She'd never been that close to a corpse.

She handed him a pair of rubber gloves, identical to the pair she'd been wearing. After putting them on, he moved to Ellison and searched for a pulse. There was no wrist pulse and no carotid pulse. Ellison was dead!

"Take his feet," he said.

"I don't want to touch him," she said.

"He won't hurt you."

"I can't," she said.

"We've come this far," he said. "We have to finish it."

She reached down and took hold of the dead man's ankles while he slid his arms under the shoulders. They carried him out of the back door. The high hedgerow in the backyard concealed their movement as they struggled with the dead weight across the lawn until they reached the side door of the garage. Once inside they dragged the body along the floor, stopping beneath one of the large beams that spanned the ceiling. They let the body fall to the floor. He kneeled beside the body and, with his gloved hand, wiped away any telltale fingerprints he might have left around the throat.

"Give me the rope," he said.

She slid the rope off her shoulder and handed it to him. He slipped the knot end over the corpse's head and pulled it tight around its neck. Then he stood and yanked on the rope several times, cinching it tight. Satisfied, he let the rope drop to the floor beside the body.

"Get the chair," he said.

She went back to the house, retrieved the folding chair, and brought it back to him. He opened the chair and placed it on its side on the floor next to the body. He stood back and looked over the area. Satisfied, he said, "Let's go."

She said, "Is that it?"

He said, "What else?"

"Aren't you going to throw the other end of the rope over the ceiling beam?"

"He weighs two-forty. We won't be able to lift him."

"It looks sloppy," she said. "And not very convincing."

"It'll work," he said.

They left out the side door. He was confident he had done everything as planned. Back inside the house, he wiped clean the bottle of whiskey and put the glass he had drunk from in his pocket. He was satisfied with the scenario he had set: a service member had suffered with a mental disability long enough. Had gotten drunk and ended his life. A logical course of events.

Before they closed the front door behind them, he wiped the doorknobs clean with his gloved hand.

In the quietness of the garage, the body twitched once, then lay motionless.

Chapter 11

Hayden Benning was pacing up and down in front of his desk like a caged tiger awaiting his next meal. "Fifty thousand dollars," he said. "And you want me to give it up?"

"What choice do you have?" I said. "You want to save your business and stop the killings, don't you?"

I was holding the letter Benning found that morning when he arrived at work. It had been shoved under his office door as the previous one had been. It contained the instructions we'd been waiting for.

Benning walked back behind his desk and dropped into his chair. "What if this is all a hoax?" he said. "Just someone trying to bleed me for the cash."

"It may be," I said. "But if you co-operate and follow our plan, whether it is will make no difference. We might catch this actor and save you money. If this blackmailer is tied to the killings, then we get two for one."

Danny and I, along with Chief Briggs, had worked out a plan to end this extortion. It was nothing unique, just the usual procedure followed by most police departments. Pay the ransom, wait undercover, watch for the perp to show, and make an apprehension. It was a practice that worked most of the time but came with no guarantees.

Benning said, "What do you want me to do?"

I referred to the letter. "They want fifty thousand in small bills placed in a manila envelope and secured with string. It's to be deposited in a mailbox on the corner of Orchard Street and Broome Street here in Manhattan. We've already checked it out.

It's one of those large mailboxes on legs with an access door you pull down. They also warn against a police presence, which is expected.

"How the hell are they gonna get the money out of a mailbox on a public street?"

"I don't know, but we'll do what they say. You'll make the drop-off. Park your car a block away and go to the corner of Orchard and Broome. Drop the envelope into the box and walk back to your car. Don't run. Don't look around or act suspicious. My partner and I will be close by. You won't see us, but we'll be watching you and the mailbox. Drive back to your office and wait till you hear from me.

"When does all this happen?"

"Midnight tomorrow. It makes sense it would happen in darkness."

At eleven thirty p.m., Danny and I parked in a service station lot across the street with an unobstructed view of the mailbox. We were parked behind a pair of gas pumps in a maroon Crown Vic. Garcia and McClusky were in a black Impala in an alley a block away. I'd instructed all patrol units to stay away from the area. The street was quiet, with almost no traffic. The corner where the mailbox stood was lit by one streetlamp. The blackmailers had chosen their location carefully.

I focused my binoculars and scanned the area. Storefronts were dark and silent. There was no movement, not even a stray cat. We were waiting for Benning to show with the drop-off money.

Danny checked his watch. "Ten minutes to midnight," he said.

The radio crackled. "Benning is on the scene," Garcia said.

I acknowledged the transmission and raised my binoculars again.

"He's out of his car, on his way to the mailbox," Garcia said.

Benning came out of the shadows and into my view. I stayed with him as he walked up the sidewalk toward the mailbox. He had the envelope under his arm.

At the mailbox, he pulled down the door and slid the envelope into the opening, letting it drop to the bottom of the box.

"That-a-boy, Hayden," I said. "Now walk away from the box."

Benning turned and walked back to his car. He gave the mailbox a second look before he got in.

"Don't look back, Hayden. Just get in the car," I said.

Benning opened the car door and slid into the driver's seat, then pulled away from the curb. We watched his taillights disappear into the darkness.

"Now we wait," Danny said.

We could hear the distant sounds of "the city that never sleeps." But where we were, the city slept. The deserted streets and the silence were ominous as we waited for our instructors to show. The night was as hot as the day. We couldn't idle the Crown Vic's engine to use the air conditioning, so we kept the windows down and hoped for a night breeze that never came.

The dash clock read 12:50. It had been almost an hour since the drop-off, but no one claimed the prize. Danny was fidgeting in his seat. He kept mopping his face and forehead with his handkerchief just to have something to do. He said, "What the hell?"

I said, "Maybe they got their nights mixed up."

I looked through my binoculars down the length of both streets on either side of the corner. There wasn't even a flickering of a shadow. I took the binoculars down and squeezed my tired eyes shut to relieve the stress. Before I opened them, Danny slapped my thigh with the back of his hand. When I looked, he pointed down Orchard Street. A dark shape was moving up the street, increasing in size as it got closer to the corner. The steady hum of an engine told me it was a motor vehicle.

Our radio crackled again. Garcia said, "Vehicle creeping along the curb on Orchard toward the box. A green four-door Honda. Two occupants. Can't ID the tag."

"We've got it," I said. "Sit tight."

The car continued on Orchard until it stopped at the curb beside the mailbox. It sat idling for almost a full minute. The soft putter from the exhaust pipe was the only sound we heard.

Danny said. "What're they waiting for?"

"There being careful," I said, "and smart."

"Let's take 'em, now," Danny said.

I said, "Not until they take possession of the money."

A figure got out of the passenger side of the car and walked to the mailbox. He was nothing more than a moving shadow. At the box, we watched him insert a key into the door lock, open the door, reach in and take the envelope, then he closed and locked the door and got back into the car. The car moved down Broome Street at a slower than normal speed. As I started the Crown Vic, I picked up the radio mic and said, "They're heading your way."

I pulled out into the street without using the headlights, but it was too dark to drive. As soon as I lit up the lights, the Honda screeched its tires and sped down Broome Street. I saw Garcia's vehicle emerge from the alley. So did they. The Honda took a hard right onto a side street. I was close behind. Garcia's headlights glared behind me. The street was narrow, with cars parked on both sides. The Honda picked up speed, squeezing between the cars, taking paint down to bare metal as it scrapped doors and side panels; throwing sparks into the darkness. It was hard for me to keep up without crunching a couple of the Crown Vic's side panels. Danny held onto the dash with a white-knuckled grip.

The Honda traveled for two more blocks before entering an empty lot between two commercial buildings. I jumped the curb and followed it across an expanse of blacktop. It turned into an alley and emerged onto the street at the other end. I maneuvered through the alley and followed it as it made a hard right at the end of the street. As I made the turn, Garcia's Impala appeared from an intersection and cut across the street in front of the Honda. The Honda's wheels screamed out of control as it tried to avoid Garcia, spewing dust into the night air. Its rear end fishtailed twice before it jumped a curb and a giant oak tree crushed its front end like a corrugated box.

I brought the Crown Vic to a jarring halt. Danny and I jumped out; guns drawn. Garcia and McClusky did the same. The passenger had opened his door and was making a run for it. He bolted down a narrow alley between two buildings. Danny ran across a lawn and disappear into the alley after him as I shoved my gun into the driver's window and said, "Show me your hands!"

The driver raised his hands. He was wearing a black leather jacket over a black sweatshirt. The sweatshirt hood covered his head. I grabbed a handful of his collar, yanked him from the vehicle, and pushed him against the rear door. "Hands on the roof!" I said. I gave him a quick pat down and ordered him to turn around. As he turned to face me, I jerked the hood from his head.

In the light of a nearby streetlamp, I was looking at the emerald green eyes of Samantha Evers.

***

It was hot in the interrogation room. We kept it that way. The overhead lamp held a hundred-watt bulb, which gave off more heat than light. Samantha Evers sat at the table, bathed by the light and feeling the heat, in more ways than one. Her eyes avoided me like a chastised child caught with her hand in a cookie jar. She slumped down with her hands in the pockets of her jeans.

"Sit up!" I said. "Like the woman you pretend to be."

She slid herself forward and placed her arms on the table.

I said, "Who else is involved in this?"

"Nobody."

"Just you and your boyfriend?"

"Yeah," she said.

"If you lie, I'll find out, and it'll make things worse for you."

"I'm not lying," she said. "Just Leon and me."

Samantha had been cuffed and arrested at the scene. They would arraign her in the morning after our initial questioning. Danny and Garcia had pursued Leon Ramos but lost him in the darkness. He had run from the scene in desperation, abandoning his girlfriend, and leaving the fifty thousand dollars in cash, which we recovered from the front seat of the Honda. We'd put out an APB on him based on a photo given to us by Samantha Evers.

"When I interviewed you, you told me your sister was Andriana Blanchet. Does she know about this?"

"Leave my sister out of this."

"Does she know?"

"No. We thought the whole thing up."

"You and Leon?"

"Yes."

"You thought you could extort money based on the murders of innocent women for your own greed."

"Leon said it was easy cash. I told him it wouldn't work. He said it would."

"Blackmail is a serious crime," I said. "You wouldn't fare well with a jury. Juries don't like blackmailers."

When she offered no reply, I said. "Did you write the ransom note?"

"Yes. Leon told me what to say."

She sat forward in her chair, suddenly concerned. "What happened to my car?"

"It's in the police impound lot crushed like a soda can."

She sat back again and said, "Tough luck."

I said, "For you. And things will get a lot tougher if you're connected to these murders."

She was silent again.

"Show me your hands," I said.

She said, "What?"

"Place your hands on the table please, and spread your fingers."

She did as I'd asked and said, "If you're checking to see if I washed—I did. Even behind my ears."

I saw nothing inordinate about her fingernails. I ignored her sarcasm and said, "Did you know Mr. Benning's partner, Mr. Ellison?"

Her hands were still on the tabletop. I said, "You can remove your hands now." She pulled them back and slid them into the pockets of her jeans again.

"I never met him," she said. "Didn't he *off* himself?"

"Shortly after the business started."

"When Benning hired me, I didn't know he had a partner."

"Does your sister know Mr. Ellison?

"She's the one who told me about him."

"What did she tell you?"

"He had a mental issue. He and Mr. Benning fought a lot over the business."

"Did your sister ever work for Mr. Benning in a capacity other than an escort?"

"Not as far as I know."

"Then how would she know a private detail like that?"

"You'd have to ask her."

"I will," I said. "If you know more than you're telling me. You can be charged as an accessory to a second crime."

"I don't know what you're talking about."

I said, "Does Leon have a job?"

"He's a mail carrier for the city. That's how he got the idea of keeping the money in a mailbox. He figured no one could get at it until he opened the box with his key."

"Your boyfriend ran and left you holding the bag," I said. "Do you know where he's headed?"

"How would I know?" she said.

"If we don't find him, you'll take the fall for this on your own," I said. You could spend a long time in jail."

"Leon will be back," she said. "I'll wait for him."

She leaned back in her chair and crossed her arms over her chest. "I want a lawyer," she said. "I'm not saying anymore."

When I got back to my desk, Danny was waiting for me. He handed me a black-and-white photo and said, "Leon Ramos' city employee ID." I looked the photo over closely. Ramos was wearing his mail carrier uniform. He was clean-shaven and well-tanned with sharp, chiseled features. His back hair was slicked back on the sides under the postal cap he wore. Danny sat in my visitor's chair and began reading from a printed sheet as I took my seat. "Leon Ramos," he said, "aged, 36, unmarried, parents deceased, no siblings. He rents rooms in So Ho and has been employed by the city as a mail carrier for the past four years.

Three hundred dollars in his bank account and owes twelve hundred on his credit card. No other outstanding debt. He's got a clean employee record and has had no run-ins with the law."

"Until now," I said.

"Guess he got stupid," Danny said.

"Let's find this guy," I said. "He might not be through being stupid."

Chapter 12

Leon Ramos lived in a second story flat above a barbershop on Canal Street. I parked a half block away and walked to number thirty-seven, which was a single entrance door blistered with dark blue paint. I opened the door and stepped into a dark hallway. It reeked of disinfectant cleaner and Bay Rum aftershave. I walked up the twenty steps to the lighted hallway at the top. I wasn't sure which apartment belonged to Ramos, so I knocked on the door to my left, where I heard a TV playing. A guy wearing a dirty t-shirt, shorts, and bedroom slippers opened the door. I said, "I'm looking for Mr. Ramos."

The guy said, "So am I. He owes me rent money." He pointed to the door behind me and said, "But he ain't in there. Hasn't been in a week."

The door behind me was open by several inches. I said, "His door's unlocked and opened."

The guy said, "He never locks it. Who's gonna steal anything from that shithole? If ya find him, let me know."

He shut his door before I could say "thanks".

The hallway was quiet enough for me to hear sounds from inside the apartment. I listened through the door but heard nothing. I knocked and waited. No answer. I push the door back and stepped inside.

The apartment was dark but for the light coming from the curtainless windows facing the street. There was a strong smell of stale cigarette smoke and whiskey. I closed the door behind me and gave the room a cursory check. I was standing in a large open room, sparsely furnished but orderly. To my left was a small kitchen. A table was cluttered with plates rancid with scraps of half-eaten food. The sink was piled high with unwashed dishes. I wrinkled my nose from the stench and moved into a small bedroom at the rear.

The window curtains were drawn, leaving the room in darkness. I flipped up the light switch to reveal an unmade double bed, its sheets and bedcoverings half hanging onto the floor. One small bed table and a chest of drawers completed the furnishings. There was a small closet in one corner. I started with that. A postal worker's uniform was hanging on a wooden hanger. Besides it hung several pairs of jeans and a pair of sweatpants. I checked the pockets, but they were empty. On the floor was a pair of black boots and a pair of well-worn running shoes. I checked the inside of each but gained only a smelly hand.

At the bedtable, I pulled open the top drawer. Inside were several porn magazines, an opened box of condoms, and a half-filled bottle of whiskey. The drawer below it was empty. An ashtray piled high with ash and cigarette butts gave off a stench that was hard to take, so I hurried to the chest of drawers. The top of the chest of drawers was cluttered with sheets of lined paper, a couple of lined notepads, and a variety of pens and pencils. One pad contained an assortment of colored paper. The top page was colored blue. I recalled Benning's ransom note was the same shade of blue. The top drawer contained underwear, t-shirts, several balled up pairs of socks, and a pair of pajamas. The drawer below it contained the jackpot. One side of the drawer held a collection of city newspapers folded to show articles relating to the moonlight murders. The papers were dated several months back. Why would Leon Ramos have such an interest in the moonlight case? Was he brushing up on the details to help launch his blackmail scheme, or was he connected to the murders?

Chapter 13

Because Chief Briggs had been taking so much heat from city hall about the moonlight murders. He called a press conference. He believed if he offered an update on the case, it would satisfy the concerns of city residents and quell the rumors of a serial killer roaming the metropolis. In addition, it would mitigate the pressure from the city fathers if they were given a verbal understanding of what the department was doing to satisfactorily solve the case.

At 9:00 a.m. Monday, we gathered on the steps of city hall under a bright sun and clear sky. I was there at Chief Briggs' request, as was Danny Nolan. There were several uniformed brass from the precinct, in addition to the Deputy Speaker and Majority Leader from the city council.

We sat on folding chairs in a semi-circle behind a wooden podium. I was wearing my best summer suit. The one Sandy said made me look thinner. Danny sat beside me, looking good in his three-piece Armani.

The major news agencies were all in attendance, waiting eagerly behind wooden barricades. There were mobile units with TV cameras mounted on their roofs and journalists waving cameras and microphones, all vying for attention. Monsignor Belducci from St. Trinity Church offered a morning prayer for the city. After a short salutation, given by the Deputy Speaker, Briggs took the podium, looking his best in his chief's regalia. His shoes were polished as bright as his brass buttons, and his uniform creases appeared sharp enough to cut steak. He wore his hat squarely on his head with the rim lowered closer to his eyes to keep from squinting into the morning sun.

When the crowd settled down, he began: "I've called you here to dispel the roomers and misinformation that's been circulating about the moonlight case. Let me assure you, at the outset, no serial killer is roaming this city."

This started rumblings from the press, which included remarks of doubt, mistrust, and dubious acceptance.

Briggs continued: "The public has a right to know and I will release information on a need-to-know basis. But I will not answer questions that may compromise the integrity of an ongoing investigation. You're all aware of the current situation, so, to expedite things, I'll begin by taking questions."

This ignited a rush of waving arms and chaotic shouting. Briggs pointed to a junior reporter near the front row. The reporter held a cell phone out to record Briggs' answer as he asked his question. "There have been several killing all in different parts of the city, which seems to point to a serial killer. Other than the fact that these women worked at the same company, do you have any other information that would tie these killings together to validate your claim that these are *not* serial murders?"

"There are avenues of pursuit that have satisfied our investigators to conclude these murders have a purpose of their own and are not random," Briggs said.

"What are those conclusions?" someone shouted from the rear.

"I can't answer that," Briggs said.

Arms waved and shouting ensued as Briggs pointed out a woman near the middle of the crowd. She pushed her way closer to the barricades and said, "Your investigation has been ongoing for a good while. It seems you're at an impasse."

Briggs retorted, "We are not at an impasse. We've uncovered several avenues which have proven fruitful."

"Can you be more specific?" someone shouted.

Briggs looked back at me. He wanted me to answer that one. The crowd simmered down as I walked to the podium. "I'm Detective Graham from Homicide," I said. "Be assured we're making progress in the case. There is no room for conjecture or misrepresentation. The facts don't lie. Although we've compiled a suspect list we are pursuing, there is nothing conclusive."

"When will you have a prime suspect?" someone yelled.

I said, "Soon."

When dealing with the press it was important to choose your words carefully. We always tried to be honest but sometimes information had to be held back without looking evasive.

A women's voice shouted the question, "Do you believe one person is doing the killings?"

Someone shouted, "What about a copycat killer?"

"A highly improbable scenario," I said. "People don't kill for no reason, other than those with deranged minds. We have explored the copycat suggestion. The evidence concludes the same person committed the crimes."

"When do you think you'll catch this guy?"

I'd had enough and turned away from the podium without answering. Chief Briggs stepped up again as someone asked, "Is the public at large in any danger?"

"We have no reason to believe these are indiscriminate killings," he said. "There is a definite motive behind them"

A voice blurted from the back row, "What's the motive?"

Briggs said, "One hasn't been established."

An older reporter wearing a wide-rim hat and sunglasses raised his hand, then asked his question. "Murders occur every day in this city," he said. "But because of the esoteric nature of these crimes shouldn't your department be handling this case in a special way rather than standard operating procedure?"

"The victims were indeed all engaged in the same profession but a crime is a crime. We handle each case according to its details. Our department uses state-of-the-art technology that has proven to be successful"

"Then why is it taking so long to find the killer?" another voice shouted.

Briggs didn't like the question. I saw it on his face. He leaned in closer to the mic and said, "Investigating a crime like this takes its own time. We put together clues one at a time until a picture emerges. Some crimes take longer to solve because of their particulars. Some are solved quicker and some are never solved. Therefore, there is no such thing as taking too long to solve a crime. We are working as expeditiously as circumstances allow."

I knew Briggs had had enough when he said, "Thank you all for coming. We will keep you abreast of our progress, as is appropriate."

Briggs had answered the questions as candidly as he could. A certain amount of information he could not or would not release and there were more than a few questions he couldn't answer.

When the conference was over, the press wasn't happy.

They never were.

Chapter 14

"Get the DA to grant her bail," I said. "If she's free, she might lead us to Ramos. "

Chief Briggs was leaning back in his desk chair, contemplating my suggestion. The look on his face told me he had become frustrated with the lack of movement in the case. On rare occasions, I had seen that look. Briggs was a seasoned cop and had learned well how to control his emotions. The press conference hadn't gone the way he'd expected. The city council and the mayor were still pushing him to end the case.

"I'll call the DA and get things rolling," Briggs said. "You and Detective Nolan keep close to her. If we're going to make this work, we need to be there at the right time.".

"See if you can get a warrant for a tap on her home phone," I said. "We'll get the info on her cell. If she tries to contact Leon Ramos, we'll know about it."

By the end of the day, they released Samantha Evers. Briggs had gotten the DA to recommend "ROR" for her. Judge Whitaker granted the "ROR" with the usual legal agreement that she shows up for her trial date. Briggs had also had Leon Ramos' apartment secured and padlocked to prevent Samantha Evers from gaining access. We tapped her apartment phone and got her cell phone information to track any calls she might make.

Since the first murder, the Moonlight Ladies Escort Service had been declining steadily. A few girls were willing to work under the circumstance but not enough to sustain the business. Samantha Evers had severed her employment with Hayden Benning and had taken a job as a server at a local diner a few blocks from her apartment. She was earning a hundred dollars a week, plus tips. A far cry from what Hayden Benning had been paying her. Her bank account showed a thousand dollars in savings and a checking account of four hundred and twenty dollars. The monthly rent on her apartment was nine-fifty. She was spread thin. Leon Ramos had closed out his account with Chase the day after he fled. Three hundred dollars wouldn't get him far.

Danny and I put in a lot of hours, keeping Samantha Evers under surveillance. Her life had become predictable. She worked during the day and returned to her apartment each evening. Grocery shopping and an occasional journey to the gym were the only times she spent outdoors. If she used her phone, it was to order takeout from the local Asian restaurant or to order a small pie from Fanelli's pizzeria on Friday nights. There was no communication between her sister or Hayden Benning and no calls from Leon Ramos. The post office was monitoring her mail; particularly out-of-town postmarks. Our communications department monitored her phone calls twenty-four-seven. If they heard anything pertinent, they'd notify us right away. A check on her lineage showed both her parents were deceased. Other than her sister (Adrianna Blanchet), there were no other siblings. She was alone in the world. Waiting for her lover, Leon Ramos, to return.

So were we!

We had no luck with the APB. Ramos had either abandoned Samantha Evers or he was lying low until the time was right to contact her. We split our around-the-clock surveillance with Garcia and McClusky. Danny and I took the day shift. Garcia and McClusky the night. *Seniority has its privileges.*

Day after day had been uneventful. Danny and I spent hours sitting in the Impala waiting and watching Samantha Evers to the point of tedium. Danny brought a deck of cards and we played

Gin Rummy on the seat between us while keeping a vigilant eye on the surroundings.

Samantha Evers never deviated from her daily routine, until one Monday, things changed. After work, she stopped at a convenience store located a block from her apartment on the street adjacent to where we had been parking. She spent less than five minutes inside and when she came out, she was carrying nothing more than the same purse she had carried in. At first, this action seemed innocuous, and we attached no importance to it. But when she went into the same store, at the same time the next day, a red flag went up. This departure from her usual routine continued each day for the rest of the week without variation. Each time, she had spent less than five minutes inside the store and come out without having made a visible purchase.

Danny said, "What could she be buying that she needs every day?"

"Whatever it is, it's small enough to conceal inside her purse or pocket," I said.

"Maybe she's got a bubble gum habit," Danny said.

I looked at my watch. It was five-forty. Garcia and McClusky were due at six to start their shift. I said to Danny, "Let's find out."

A small bell attached to the doorframe jingled as I opened the door and stepped inside. The place was cluttered with piles of magazines and newspapers. Shelves of candy filled the front counter, behind which hung streamers of New York City Lottery rub-offs like party decorations. On a wall behind the counter, an assortment of tobacco products was displayed: cigarettes, cigars, and tins of pipe tobacco. Beside it, a large coffee machine held a carafe of steaming brew. The place smelled of coffee, tobacco, and newspaper ink.

A woman wearing a white apron was behind the counter. Her blonde hair was pinned back into a ponytail. She looked to be about Samantha's age. A small silver crucifix on a chain around her neck reflected the sun coming through the plate-glass window. When we approached, she offered a smile. I showed her my shield and said, "Are you the owner?"

She said, "My husband and I are. What can I do for you?"

I asked her about the girl who came into her store at the same time every day for the past week.

She said, "You mean, Samantha? The girl with the tattoo?"

I said, "Yes. How well do you know her?"

"She's been a customer of ours for several years," she said. "Lives in the neighborhood. Although I haven't seen her lately."

"Until she started stopping in every day after work since last Monday," I said.

Danny said, "Why would she do that?"

The woman became suddenly reticent. She began straightening items on the countertop, trying to ease her discomfort at the question.

"Is there a problem with my question?" Danny said.

"I-I don't want to get involved in something I shouldn't be," she said.

Danny said, "I think you should tell us what you know."

She looked through a doorway into a small back room, then indicated for us to follow her. The room was used for storage. Its perimeter walls were stacked high with cardboard boxes. A round table and four chairs had been squeezed into the center. A kid wearing overalls was sweeping between the boxes as we entered.

"Jimmy, please watch the store front," the woman. said.

Jimmy leaned his broom against the doorframe and walked out into the store without a word. We took seats at the table. The woman collected her thoughts and said, "My name is Aggie Woolrich. My husband and I own this place. On Monday, an envelope was delivered here, but to the attention of Samantha

Evers. I thought little of it, so I waved Samantha in as she walked by the store that afternoon after work, and gave it to her."

"What was her reaction?" Danny said.

"She seemed surprised, but accepted the envelope, put it into her purse, and thanked me. As I said. I thought nothing of it until a second letter showed up on Thursday."

"Someone addressed it here but intended it for Samantha Evers," Danny said.

"Yes. Like the first one."

"Did you notice from where it had been mailed?" I said.

"No. I put it in a drawer behind the counter and waited to give it to Samantha that afternoon."

"Didn't you wonder why someone was mailing letters to Samantha Evers via your address?"

"I did, but I didn't want to question Samantha about it. There was no harm being done."

"How many envelopes like that did you receive since Monday?"

"There was the first one on Monday and then another on Thursday."

"Did you give her the one you received on Thursday?"

"Yes. She stopped in after work."

"And she's been stopping in every day after work since Monday?"

"She wanted to see if other envelopes had arrived."

"Did she discuss the envelopes with you?" Danny said.

"No. Each day, she'd ask if any new mail had arrived for her. If there was none, she'd thank me and leave."

"Have you told your husband about the letters?" I said.

"No. I didn't think it was important."

I took Leon Ramos' picture from my pocket and showed it to her. "Do you know this man?" I said.

She looked at it and said, "Could be Samantha's boyfriend, but it's hard to tell with that hat on."

"Do you know him?"

"She's been in here with him a few times, but I don't know him. He buys cigarettes and magazines. Once he bought a pack of gum. I've never spoken to him."

"You seem to remember a lot about him, yet you can't possibility identify him from the photo."

"I see faces all day," she said. "I'm more concerned with what people buy from us."

I took the photo from her and said, "We're going to need your help, Mrs. Woolrich."

She looked apprehensive, almost afraid. "I don't want to get involved with the law," she said. "My husband and I are peaceful people."

"You won't have to do much," I said. "And it would be a big help to us."

"What do you want me to do?"

"If you receive another letter for Samantha, don't tell her about it."

I handed her my card. "Keep it safe, call me at that number, and wait until I get here."

She looked at the card, then at me, and said, "What do I do if she asks if there's a letter for her?"

"Tell her, no," I said.

"You're asking me to lie."

"We're asking you to help."

There was an awkward silence between us. I wasn't sure what to say. I didn't want to debase her religious compass in the name of serving justice. Danny had nothing to offer. I stood there searching for the words to justify our request until Danny said. "This isn't an exercise in morality, Mrs. Woolrich. You may be helping us save lives."

She reached up and impulsively rubbed the crucifix between her thumb and forefinger as if seeking atonement for a sin she hadn't yet committed.

"Is that all you want me to do?"

"That's all," I said.

"Okay," she said.

Before we left, I said, "I feel lucky. I'll take five dollars' worth of rub-offs and a chocolate bar."

Danny said, "You can tear off five for me too."

She tore off the cards, took our money, and said, "Good luck."

I thanked her for her cooperation and we left.

Back in the Impala, I unwrapped the chocolate bar. It was the kind I'd enjoyed as a kid. The ones with the almonds inside.

I said. "Ramos is communicating with his girlfriend through this convenience store. A clever move."

"Guess he's not through with her," Danny said.

"Let's hope he keeps sending her love letters," I said. "They'll lead us right to him."

"Or lead *him* to his end," Danny said.

I wasn't sure what Danny meant, and he saw it on my face.

He said, "It's in every love story ever written. The guy winds up dead because of the love he has for his woman."

I held my look as Danny continued. He said: "You know: Romeo and Juliet, Cyrano De Bergerac, Antony and Cleopatra, even King Kong died because of the woman he loved."

And then he added, in his best Shakespearean voice, "Love is the sweetness of life."

I broke the chocolate bar in two and gave him half.

CHAPTER 15

We kept up our vigil throughout the weekend. The following Monday brought nothing out of the ordinary. There was no success with the APB. Samantha Evers followed her daily routine to the letter. Watching her was bordering on monotony. Danny brought a deck of playing cards and we resorted to playing Gin Rummy to abate the tedium. I spread my cards on the seat and said, “Gin!”

Danny said, “That’s three in a row for you. Show me your sleeves.”

I smiled, gathered up the cards, and was about to re-shuffle when my cell phone buzzed. It was Aggie Woolrich. She said, “Detective Graham, I have what you’ve been waiting for. It arrived a few minutes ago.”

I said, “I’ll be right there,” and ended the call.

“She’s got one,” I said to Danny. “Be right back.”

After Aggie Woolrich gave me the delivered letter, I thanked her again and went back to the car. I slid behind the wheel and held the envelope up for Danny to see. He read the hasty scrawl and the postmark stamp, and said, “Harlem. He’s been under our noses all the time.”

I said, “How far could he have gone on three hundred dollars?”

On the way back to headquarters, Danny phoned Chief Briggs to inform him we had the item we’d been waiting for. Following protocol and being the stickler, Briggs was for adhering to the law. He said he’d get a warrant for the contents "to cover our asses." By the time we got to Briggs' office, he had a warrant signed by Judge Whitaker on his desk.

I handed the envelope to Briggs. He gave it back to me and said, "You open it."

I peeled back the gummed flap and removed a folded piece of paper. The words were written in uppercase block letters on white paper. The note was brief and to the point.

I handed the note to Danny and said to Briggs; "Ramos wants her to meet him tomorrow at the Port Authority Bus Terminal at 10:00 a.m. It's obvious he's planning on grabbing a bus and heading out of town with her. He asks her to bring whatever amount of money she can and a change of clothes for him."

"Where is this meeting to take place?"

"Lower level.".

"Nothing more specific?"

"He instructed her not to look for him and that he'll find her."

Briggs took the note from Danny and read it. Then said. "We'll be waiting for them."

We sat down with Chief Briggs and planned the operation that afternoon. Danny suggested that he and I handled things alone, since we could identify Samantha Evers and Leon Ramos without question. Briggs saw it differently.

Danny and I would take the lead. Uniformed officers in street clothes would cover all the entrances and exits on the ground floor and at locations for outgoing buses. Everyone would be issued a photo I.D. of the suspects and wear an earpiece/microphone for communication purposes.

We would not notify the Port Authority of any police activity. Those involved would arrive at their designated locations at various times in the morning so as not to show an unusual police presence. Firearms were to be used only in self-defense.

Unmarked vehicles would be used for transportation. Briggs himself would be in plain clothes overseeing the entire operation.

Danny had been listening to Briggs' instructions without comment, until he said, "Maybe we should tamp down the operation."

"In what way, detective?" Briggs said.

"I think we're overextending ourselves," Danny said. "Like hitting a fly with a sledgehammer. Our suspects are charged with blackmail and extortion. It's not like they're public enemy numbers one and two. We might step on each other's toes if there are too many of us. I think we'd have greater success if Detective Graham and I handled it alone."

"Our suspects might be the killers of the moonlight ladies," Briggs said. "Did you forget about that, detective?"

Danny didn't answer.

My sentiments were with Danny, but I remained quiet. I knew Briggs was staunch in his decision making. Engaging in negotiation was futile. Danny knew it, too.

"I'm not taking any chances that this guy slips away again," Briggs said. "We'll do it my way."

We put the operation into effect at 8:00 a.m. the following morning. It was Briggs' order to arrive at the terminal early since Ramos might get the idea to leave on an earlier bus with Samantha Evers should she show up before ten.

I parked the Chevy a block away from the terminal. Danny and I walked through the eighth Avenue entrance at 8:15. I wore my brown suit and carried an empty leather briefcase. Danny wore jeans, a short-sleeved pullover shirt, and a Yankee's ball cap. He carried a backpack stuffed with crumpled newspapers across his shoulders.

The main promenade was crowded with the usual early morning commuters. Danny and I split up and waited on either side of the front entrance. Briggs had sent Garcia and McClusky to Samantha Evers's apartment. At 9:05, we heard through our earpiece that Samantha Evers had gotten into a cab at the front of her apartment building. Garcia and McClusky were following the cab close as it made its way toward the terminal.

At 9:30, Samantha Evers walked through the 8th Avenue entrance. She was wearing a gray sweatsuit with a red stripe running along the arms and legs. It was an advantage for us and a mistake for her. She stuck out like a barber pole. The large canvas bag she carried was weighted, and she struggled to keep it on her shoulder.

Unaware of our presence, she hurried past us down to the main level promenade. Danny and I followed.

In police work, there are two ways to tail someone; covertly or deliberately. The first strategy is obvious. The second keeps a suspect off balance, knowing they're being followed, always looking over his or her shoulder. Each strategy is devised to achieve a certain outcome. Danny and I kept our distance but always had Samantha Evers in sight.

She made her way through the commuter crowd and took the first elevator to the lower level.

Through my earpiece, I said to Danny, "She's going down."

Danny said, "I'll take the stairs."

I waited for her to reach the bottom, then stepped onto the elevator behind her. When I reached the lower level, Danny emerged from the stairwell. He let me get a short distance ahead of him, then continued behind me. At the lower level, she walked past several gate numbers but didn't stop until she reached a bench in front of a Hudson newsstand. She took a seat and placed her canvas bag on the bench beside her. She kept looking into the crowd for Leon Ramos. There had been no sign of him. When I checked the wall clock, it read: 10:16.

Ramos was late!

I scanned the crowd but didn't see Ramos. Samantha Evers was fidgeting on the bench. She was, no doubt, apprehensive and unsure of what to expect. I watched her unzip her canvas bag and remove a small purse. She slid out a stack of bills and counted them. When she was through, she counted them a second time, returned them to her purse, and zipped the bag closed.

Through my earpiece, I heard an officer report to Briggs. He had identified Leon Ramos, who had entered the terminal at the 40th Street entrance. Ramos was wearing jeans and a black sweatshirt. Briggs repeated his order to follow Ramos, but not to detain him. With a quick hand wave, Danny let me know he'd heard the transmission. He removed the backpack from his shoulders and let it drop to the floor. A sign he was expecting a foot chase.

I stepped behind a marble pillar and waited for Ramos to show up. It wasn't long before he did. When he appeared to Samantha Evers from out of the crowd, she rushed to him and wrapped her arms around him. He pushed her away, took her hand, and hurried with her down the promenade. Danny moved away from his vantage point and followed them. He was closer to them than I was.

I said into my earpiece, "Detectives Nolan and Graham have the suspects in visual proximity, headed West on the lower level."

Danny crossed the promenade to my side and began a slow jog to keep up with them. I left my briefcase where I was, picked up my pace, and followed Danny. Samantha and her boyfriend were weaving through the crowd at a considerable pace. Ramos still had a hold of Samantha's hand. She was having a hard time keeping up with him, clutching the canvas bag with one hand and hanging onto Ramos with the other. She lost her balance several times and tumbled to the floor. Ramos yanked her to her feet so he could keep up his pace. Danny was moving fast and closing in on them. It was difficult dodging commuters, trying not to knock one to the floor, or getting knocked down myself. It was like being in a cattle yard.

I said into my earpiece, "Give 'em some room, Danny. They can't get far."

Danny didn't hear or was too wrapped up in the chase. I went into a quick jog. As I got closer, I saw Leon Ramos look behind him. Recognizing Danny, he released Samantha's hand and bolted into a full run, leaving her to fall to the floor. As Danny stopped to help her to her feet, I ran past them without breaking stride and found myself the lone pursuer. Ramos was at least twenty feet ahead of me. He was younger and quicker than me, which made it tougher for me to keep up. I remembered the breathing routine I'd learned at college when I ran track. It worked for me then. It would work for me now.

I counted my breaths as I ran and poured it on. Leon Ramos was less than ten feet ahead of me now. I was sure I had him until he jumped a turnstile and ran into a smaller promenade. There was less foot traffic here, but it didn't make running easier. I pushed myself harder and got close enough to where I could reach out for him. When he looked back to see if I was gaining on him, I grabbed his collar and yanked him down. We hit the floor together. I brought my knee up to his chest and kept it there. His hands came up around my throat. When he applied pressure, I threw a hard right into his jaw. He didn't flinch, so I followed it with a left. His eyeballs rolled up behind his lids and his hands melted away from my throat.

I yanked him up to his feet. He was breathing hard. So was I. Through the mask of perspiration on his face, a red nodule was already turning purple under his left eye.

When I removed my handcuffs from my belt, I made an amateur mistake. I took my eyes off him. Ramos used the opportunity to drive his fist into my midsection. I buckled forward and held my stomach as he ran into a nearby stairwell leading up to the main floor. I fought to get air back into my lungs as I shouted into my earpiece, "Ramos is heading up to the main floor!"

While I waited for my breath to return, Danny ran up behind me. He had Samantha Ever in handcuffs. He said, "You okay?"

I nodded.

"What happened?"

"He sucker punched me and ran up that stairwell."

Samantha Evers looked in the stairwell's direction. Her face was hard with anger and disappointment. She said, "That's the second time he left me behind."

A manhunt began that afternoon for Leon Ramos. Every officer involved had been alerted to his escape. Chief Briggs decided to keep Samantha Evers free without bail since she was our only connection to Ramos. We kept her under twenty-four-seven surveillance, hoping Ramos would try a second time to contact her.

Chapter 16

The heatwave broke by the end of the week. A tidal wave of cool air rolled across the city, bringing renewed life to its inhabitants. Sandy and I had resumed our morning jogs around the lake at Oakwood Park, now that the heat and the maple syrup were gone. We did our usual twice around the lake, then sat on a bench for a breather. Sandy removed her water bottle from her belt, took a sip, then handed it to me. I took a long drink and said, "It's nice to breathe again."

"And enjoy the outdoors," Sandy said.

"And together," I said.

She smiled and rubbed my cheek.

We sat without speaking, listening to the sounds of summer and enjoying the sunshine and gentle breeze that blew rippling waves across the water. It was the quintessential summer day. A group of kids was operating a remote-controlled sailboat on the other side of the lake. From where I sat, I heard them arguing over whose turn would be next.

There were more dog walkers on the path than usual. A small terrier on a leash began yapping at a Labrador Retriever as they approached each other. The terrier pulled on its leash, snapping and snarling in a fierce display of hostility. The Retriever ignored the advances and walked nobly, but warily, beside its owner. I wondered what the terrier would have done if either dog hadn't been on a leash.

At the end of the lake, the ice cream vender was attending to a long line of customers. He had been a fixture at the lake. Sandy and I had purchased lots of ice cream from him over the years. We'd learned the names of every flavor he offered, but strangely, we'd never learned *his* name. He was always, "the ice-cream vender."

As I continued looking out over the water, I thought of Ruth Ellison and the heartache she had endured since her husband's murder.

Sandy said, "What are you thinking about?"

I said, "I'm thinking about you."

"No, you're not," she said. "You're bringing your work home again. Something's bothering you."

"I was thinking about the sorrows I see in people," I said.

"That's something inherent in your profession," Sandy said. "Something you should've learned to handle by now."

"I handle it," I said, "but one never stops feeling for people's despair. You're supposed to help, but sometimes there's nothing you can do."

"You can't be the conscience of the world."

"I'm not trying to be. I'm just trying to justify my conscience. Trying to bring into focus the fuzzy area between right and wrong."

"Sometimes a person has to do something wrong, or bad to accomplish something right, or good," Sandy said. "Especially in your profession. You're only human. Doing your *best* is itself your reward. What's troubling you now?"

"Ruth Ellison believes her husband was murdered, didn't take his own life."

"She's the wife of Benning's former partner?"

"Yes. She came to me for help. I don't want to let her down. But if the facts prove her husband killed himself; I'll be the bearer of the truth. And she'll have to live with that truth for the rest of her life."

"And she will accept that truth and live with it."

"Maybe."

"Do you have evidence to corroborate her claim?"

"The official reports conclude it was suicide."

"Then tell her that."

"I did, but she wouldn't accept it. She pleaded with me to dig deeper."

"You'll do what's right," Sandy said.

"Then there's Ashley Allan," I said. "She works in an environment of fear every day, after having overheard Benning's phone call. She imagines him as a probable murderer, a criminal, a monster. There were no words of reassurance I could've given her to make her feel safe. It's up to me to prove or disprove the claims of these two women."

"Cops aren't always heroes, Max, despite what some people may think. Is there any connection between Ellison's death and the moonlight killings?"

"Nothing conclusive."

"You'll find the answers. You always do."

"But will I find the answer to the key question?"

"Which is?"

"Who's killing the Moonlight Ladies?

I dug deeper into Andriana Blanchet's history. She had neglected to tell me she had a sister working for Benning. I wondered why she'd kept that from me and what other pertinent information she might have withheld.

The city clerk's office for the city of New York provided all the information I needed. Andriana Blanchet (nee Evers) was born in New York City and attended NYU, where she met and married Charles Blanchet. The marriage ended in divorce after three plus years. After which she fortuitously ran into her old boyfriend, Hayden Benning, who offered her a place in his newly formed business. Most of what I found validated what Adrianna Blanchet had told me during our interview. But she had left out one relevant fact. According to the city record, she and Hayden Benning had tied the knot a year after she began working for him. The record maintained they were still married.

There was nothing in McCluskey's report that stated Benning had married and neither Benning nor Blanchet had offered that information. It was time for me to confront Benning.

***

The outer office of the Moonlight Ladies was deserted when I entered. Ashley Allan was in her usual position behind her desk, tapping her keyboard. As I approached her desk, she said, "Detective Graham, without looking up.

I said, in a low voice, "Hello, Ashley. How are you?"

She said, "I'm glad you're here."

I could see the consternation on her face. I said, "Is something wrong?"

She shook her head and said, "He's waiting for you."

She was doing her best to deal with an uncomfortable situation.

I knocked on Benning's door and went in. He was staring out his windows with his arms behind his back. He wasn't wearing his suit jacket and his shirtsleeves were rolled up to his elbows. When I approached his desk, he turned and said, "Your call sounded ominous. What's the problem?"

He walked back behind his desk but didn't sit. I stood where I was.

"The problem is you," I said.

He gave me that phony look of confusion I had seen before.

"I don't understand," he said.

"You lied to me," I said. "I don't like being lied to."

He sat in his chair and loosened his tie, giving himself time to think about what to say. "I'm not sure what you mean," he said.

"Don't play with me, Benning," I said.

"What are you getting at?" he said.

"Why you didn't tell me you're married to Adrianna Blanchet?"

The look on his face revealed neither surprise nor concern. But rather a mask of guilt at having been caught in a lie.

He removed the bottle of whiskey from his desk drawer and poured himself a shot, searching for the words to fabricate an explanation. When he raised the glass to his lips, I checked out his fingernails. They were polished and manicured, but no longer than what I would consider normal for a man in his position. He drained his glass, then said, "I didn't think that information was pertinent."

"Everything's pertinent to a murder investigation," I said.

"How'd you find out?"

"A matter of public record. Did you think you could keep it from me?"

"I suppose I should have told you."

"You need to come clean with me or I'll ask Chief Briggs to take me off this case and assign another detective."

"I wouldn't want that," he said.

He poured another shot and knocked it back. "Okay," he said. "Adrianna and I married three years ago. There was no reason to keep it a secret other than we thought it would present a better picture to the ladies if they thought they were working for a bachelor."

"What difference would it have made?"

"The business was in its infancy. We were struggling to keep it alive and doing everything we could to make it work. We were learning as we went along. It was Adrianna's idea. Believe me, there is nothing more to it."

"Your wife didn't tell me she had a sister, and that she's employed by you. You also left that part out of our interview."

"I hardly know Samantha," he said. "We don't get along well. She's too immature for this job. I only hired her because of Adrianna."

"Does your wife have what would be considered a normal relationship with her sister?"

"I guess so."

"You're not sure?"

"As I said, I don't know Samantha well."

"Then I'll need to talk to your wife."

"Why?"

"It was her sister that sent you that ransom letter."

The disbelief on his face seemed genuine. He poured himself another drink from the bottle but, as a second thought, poured the liquid back into the bottle, capped it, and placed it in his desk drawer.

"Samantha and her boyfriend devised the plan," I said. "She knew about the murders and used them as leverage to extort money from you."

"Are they connected to the murders?"

"Don't know yet."

"Why would Samantha do such a thing?"

"Maybe your wife knows."

"That's crazy. Why would Adrianna involve herself in that?

I didn't offer my opinion and let him wonder about that himself. She was *his* wife.

I said, "How involved was your partner in making business decisions?"

"Mike had some good ideas," he said.

"Did you get along with Mike?"

"We disagreed occasionally over business decisions, but Mike and I were more than partners. We were friends, service buddies."

"Do you believe he took his own life?"

"No reason not to. Mike had problems that nobody could fix. His death was a shocker, but we accepted it as inevitable."

"His wife doesn't accept it."

"What do you mean?"

"She believes her husband was murdered. She's asked for my help. I'm looking into it."

"Why would anybody want to murder Mike?" he said.

***

The following morning, I went to see Adrianna Blanchet. She answered her door with a perfunctory smile and said, "I thought I answered all your questions, detective?"

I said, "Not quite."

She led me to her living room and offered me a seat on the sofa where I'd questioned her before. This time, I remained standing. "I've been to see your husband," I said.

She shot me a surprised look.

"I know you and Hayden are married," I said.

She carried the surprised look to the bar, thinking about what she wanted to say. I waited while she mixed herself a drink. She didn't offer me one.

She brought her glass to the sofa and sat. "I was foolish to keep it from you," she said. "It's been a secret of Hayden's and mine for so long I thought it was secure."

"Your sister's been arrested," I said.

Another surprised look.

"The sister you also forgot to tell me about."

She took a large drink from her glass

"Why was she arrested?"

"For blackmailing your husband. Did you know he was being blackmailed?"

"I did," she said. "Of course, I couldn't mention it. But I didn't know Samantha was involved. I can't believe my sister would do a thing like that?"

"Her boyfriend Leon planned it and she went along with it. They saw it as easy money. "

"Are they a part of the moonlight killings?"

"Maybe."

"Samantha doesn't have that in her."

"Anyone can commit murder if they're driven by circumstance."

"Not Samantha," shc said.

She took another long drink, then said, "Maybe her boyfriend killed those women."

"Maybe he did. And maybe your sister helped him. Do you know Leon?"

"No. I don't see Samantha often enough to be a part of her life. What will happen to her now?"

"If she's indicted for blackmail and extortion, she'll stand trial. But if she's a part of the killings, she's just as guilty as her boyfriend, whether she did the actual killing or not. And she'll hang next to him."

She winced and said, "Do you have to say it like that?"

"It's the consequence of their actions," I said.

"Will she go to jail?"

"If she's found guilty.

"Is there anything I can do?"

"To help her?"

"Yes."

"I don't think so. Unless you know something I don't know. If you do, tell me."

"I only know what you just told me about it."

"Then there's nothing you can do. If I were you, I'd worry about my own credibility. You haven't earned much of that with me."

CHAPTER 17

Danny and I took a ride to Victoria Quinlan's place in Prospect Heights. She had phoned me to tell me she had remembered something concerning George DeMarco, but didn't want to discuss it over the phone. I told her I'd be there as soon as I could.

The sun was setting behind a row of brownstones, painting the facades of the buildings a golden yellow. The neighborhood was quiet but for a group of kids playing baseball in the middle of the street. Something you saw little of these days. The internet had all but eradicated that youthful activity. *American's pastime had passed.*

I found a parking spot a half block away, and we walked the distance to the Quinlan brownstone. We climbed the brick steps to the front door.

I rang the doorbell and waited.

No answer.

When there was no response on the second ring, Danny said, "How long ago did she phone you?"

I said, "Just after three."

Danny checked his watch. "It's been almost an hour," he said.

I peered through the glass pane in the door. The vestibule was dark. Danny tried the knob, and the door opened. He pushed the door back, and we stepped in. The inner door in the vestibule leading to the main room had been left open about six inches. I called, "Miss Quinlan. It's Detective Graham."

When there was no answer, we opened the inner door and went in. The main living area appeared undisturbed. It was conventionally furnished, with a three-cushion sofa, two upholstered armchairs, and a glass coffee table. The window curtains were opened fully, allowing in the rays of the afternoon sun. A laptop computer on a small desk against one wall was playing a string arrangement.

I said, "Beethoven."

Danny said, "E.L.O."

He shut the computer down, then went to check the kitchen while I headed for the bedroom. The drawn curtains kept the bedroom in semi-darkness. Despite the bed cover having been turned down, the bed hadn't been slept in.

To my left was a small bathroom. The door was partially open. I called Victoria Quinlan's name again as I pushed the door back with my foot, leaned in, and flipped up the light switch. There was a toothbrush, toothpaste, and hair brush on the sink. A frosted glass door enclosed the bathtub to my right. I could see irregular shapes of dark and light behind it. Although water dripped from the shower head into the tub, the room didn't feel steamy or moist, and the vanity mirror wasn't fogged over, which told me the shower had not been used recently

I recalled how in those old detective movies they often discovered a mysterious corpse in the bathtub. The victim was usually a guy who'd been stabbed multiple times, his eyes wide, staring up from beneath the red soapy water in true to life Hollywood technicolor. More often, it was a young woman who'd slit her wrists to effect vengeance on her unfaithful lover. If it was a five-star picture, one might find two bodies entangled in a tender embrace after mutually consenting to end their lives in the name of eternal love.

Hollywood had a knack for linking love with death.

I had seen death in many forms over the years, including bathtub corpses, which are the ugliest of images you don't soon forget. I held the door handle and hoped I wouldn't see another. I took a deep breath, slid the door open, and looked into the tub.

There was a bar of soap, and a back brush in a pool of sudsy water at the bottom, but no mysterious corpse.

When I walked back into the living room, Danny was standing behind the sofa. He pointed to the floor in front of him. I stepped around the sofa and saw Samantha Quinlan lying on the carpet in a semi-fetal position. Her face was chalk white.

She was wearing a cotton bathrobe and one bedroom slippers. The other slipper was on the floor beside her.

Danny said, “She’s dead.”

I kneeled beside her and saw the now familiar bruising around her neck and the skin indentation on the front of her throat.

The moonlight murderer had claimed another victim.

We did a cursory check of the rest of the apartment. Nothing looked out of place. Upon inspection of the front doors, we saw no indication of forced entry.

Danny said, “She must’ve known her killer and let him in.”

On the coffee table in front of the sofa, I noticed an ashtray with the remains of a half-smoked cigar. Danny saw it, too. He said, “Miss Quinlan must’ve had a new boyfriend.”

“Or a closet habit,” I said.

I took my handkerchief from my pocket and picked the cigar out of the ashtray. It had a short ash left on its front end and chew marks on its opposite end. The band had been untouched. The label read: “Montecristo, Habana”. George DeMarco had smoked the same brand of cigar the day we visited him at his office.

I dropped the cigar in an evidence bag and put it into my pocket. Danny called in the homicide and we waited until the coroner and forensics arrived. Chief Briggs showed up unexpectedly. He surveyed the scene and said to me, “Another moonlight?”

I said, “Just like the others.”

“How many does this make?”

I said, "Five

"What's the MO?"

"Identical in each case," I said. "Strangulation. No signs of a struggle or wounds, other than markings on the throat."

"Must be a big guy to overpower these women without a struggle," Briggs said.

"It doesn't take much strength to incapacitate someone when they're fighting for air," Danny said. "If you get a good grip and squeeze, the struggle is over quickly."

There was frustration and dissatisfaction on Briggs' face from having gained little evidence to advance the case. I showed him the evidence bag containing the cigar. "This could be a connection to our person of interest, George DeMarco."

Briggs said, "The guy with a malignant attitude toward women? What's the connection?"

"We found this in an ashtray on the coffee table. DeMarco smokes this brand. It's an expensive Cuban make. Not one the average joe smokes. If we can match DNA or prints, it'll put DeMarco at the crime scene."

Briggs said, "Why would DeMarco come here to Quinlan's apartment?"

"Their relation was volatile," Danny said. "Maybe things went too far, and this is the result."

"Maybe," I said. "But there's no forced entry. Why would she let DeMarco in if she feared him as she told me?"

"And why would he stay long enough to enjoy a cigar?" Briggs said.

Chapter 18

My mother celebrated her Italian heritage with pride, although she had been American born and raised and was proud of it. She said being an American was special. It's an exceptional place to live. She liked to kid me about being half-Italian. She'd say, "Being half Italian is better than none."

Our family name, "Graham", originates from the town of "Grantham" in the county of Lincolnshire, England, which is my father's ancestry. My mother told us the name means. "warlike child", which suited my brother Vinnie and me since we were always scrapping with each other when we were youngsters.

My mother had invited Sandy and me to her house for Sunday dinner. Since the passing of my father, my mother hadn't had the desire to cook much, but occasionally, I could convince her to put together a meal for me and that made us both happy. Spending time with my mother allowed me to forget about my work and enjoy the everyday pleasures of normal family life. The only time I enjoyed more was when I visited my daughters.

My mother lived with my aunt Theresa, her sister, in the same house where I grew up. When Uncle Carlo died (aunt Theresa's husband), Aunt Theresa moved in with my mother. Since Marlene moved the grandkids to South Jersey and my younger brother Vinnie left for Arizona to sell real estate, I tried to ease my mother's loneliness by visiting her as much as I could.

She couldn't understand why Vinnie left. He'd been living at home with a "come and go" lifestyle. But his meager real estate following was taking him nowhere, and his dream of bigger and better things had been eating away at him for a long time. He'd hung on to a selfish priority and felt the time for a career change was right. When the opportunity arose for him to sell land in Arizona, he jumped on it.

Inhaling the smoke from three packs of cigarettes a day for sixty years, put my father in an early grave. After he died, his doctor told me his lungs looked like a piece of burned toast, a difficult analogy to accept about one's own father's medical condition. An uneducated man who rarely touched alcohol, he did his best to keep his family happy, but sometimes the constraints of ignorance made it difficult for him to make the right decisions. He worked hard to support his family. His meager income offered no time or money for vacations away from home. I can't recall one trip we took as a family that included a car ride. While our schoolmates were flying with their families to Disneyland and Magic Mountain, my brother Vinnie and I were consigned to fishing trips with our father to the muddy banks of the Passaic River, less than two miles from our home. Although most times we enjoyed ourselves, it wasn't Disneyland.

My mother loved my father in the only way she knew how, as he had loved her in his own genuine but meager way. He treated my brother and me with as much understanding and love as he knew how to give, and that's the way I've chosen to remember him.

We arrived at the house on Sandford Street around five o'clock. I shut off the Chevy's engine and sat in the driveway and stared up at the old place.

Sandy said, "I see nostalgia on your face."

"A lot of great memories were made here," I said.

We got out and stood under the old oak tree in the front yard. My father had tied a rope around the large horizontal branch for Vinnie and me to swing out over the sidewalk. There was a dark abrasion where the rope had worn away some of the bark.

We walked up the wooden steps onto the porch. The vintage milk pail my father had spray painted a bright silver was still standing beside the front door. Its finish had long ago weathered to a dull gray. He had stenciled the number 102 on the front of the can with black paint. I recalled how proud he'd been of his trophy, so much so, that he had secured it to the front porch floor with a chain and padlock and half-inch lag screws. My mother wanted to place flowers in it. But he wouldn't let her. He said it would be sacrilege. The milk pail was a piece of Americana that you don't see anymore.

I took out my key, but pressed the doorbell instead, to give my mother a sense of self-worth. She opened the door wearing that warm smile that had always been her testament to her love for us. At seventy-six, she'd kept herself in pretty good shape. Her dyed black hair was kept as she had always worn it and looked good against her olive complexion. She wore a powder blue blouse over blue jeans and white sneakers. A yellow apron had been tied around her ample waist with a bow.

She said, "Sandra, I'm so glad to see you." She took Sandy's hand and kissed her cheek. Then leaned over and gave me a hug and kiss.

My mother regarded Sandy as her daughter-in-law, although we hadn't tied the knot. She hoped Sandy and I would marry and provide her with a grandson. Even though she loved her granddaughters obsessively, "a grandson would complete the package," she'd say.

"It's good to see you, Mrs. G," Sandy said. Sandy had begun calling my mother "Mrs. G" after hearing Danny Nolan refer to her in the same way. My mother liked the intimacy of the moniker and accepted it without objection.

We followed my mother into the dining room. The house smelled delicious of warm bread and spices and brought back memories of the many holidays our family had enjoyed together.

"Sit," my mother said. "The meal is ready. There's wine on the table."

The dining table had been set, with "the good dishes and silverware" that had always been kept in the breakfront and used only on holidays, or when my mother's brother, Uncle Angelo, and his wife, Aunt Rosa came to visit from California.

Sandy and I took seats at the side of the table, allowing my mother to sit at the head, which had been my father's place. I opened the bottle of Zinfandel and filled Sandy's glass and mine. Although my mother didn't drink alcohol, I put an inch in her glass so she wouldn't feel left out.

My mother came out of the kitchen balancing a large dish of lasagna. She said, "Just the way Sandra likes it."

I took the dish from her and set it at the center of the table. The red sauce glistened under the light of the chandelier just as I remembered it as a kid. The great aroma of oregano sprinkled on the top layer made my nostrils flare.

"Let me help," Sandy said. She followed my mother into the kitchen and carried back an enormous bowl of *insalata*. The romaine lettuce was garnished with black olives and anchovies, just the way I like it.

Mama knows best.

My mother cradled two loaves of homemade Italian bread in her arms. She placed them on a cutting board on the table and cut the warm bread into even pieces. Wisps of steam rose as the bread knife cut through the golden crust.

My mother took her seat only after she had set everything to her satisfaction.

"Ma. You've outdone yourself with this meal," I said.

"I know how much Sandy loves my lasagna." She said. "Have some bread."

I cut squares of lasagna and placed them in each of our dishes. My mother went to the kitchen and brought back a plate of sweet sausage and meatballs. "I almost forgot these," she said.

Sandy speared a meatball. I snagged two and a sausage.

As we ate, I kept thinking about how happy my mother looked. This is what she lived for; taking care of her family and making us happy. If Vinnie and my daughters had been at the table, my mother would have been beside herself with joy. But life rearranges things for another purpose.

We had been enjoying the meal over small talk until my mother said, "I saw on TV about the *moonglow* murders."

I said, "Moonlight."

"Who's doing this to these women, Maxwell?"

"Ma. I don't want to talk about my work," I said. "I came here to relax."

"I know," my mother said. She reached over and pinched my cheek. "But this is such a terrible thing. All those young girls were killed. Can you make it stop, Maxwell?"

"We're working on it, Ma. It'll stop."

"After how many more lives are taken?" my mother said.

I put my fork down on my napkin and said, "Can we enjoy this meal and talk about something else?"

She looked at Sandy while directing her words to me. "You've got a young woman yourself to worry about."

Sandy said, "I don't think I've anything to be concerned about, Mrs. G. These crimes are isolated and have their own purpose."

"Such a thing," my mother said. "When I was young, nothing like this ever happened."

"It did, Ma. You just didn't hear about it. Events travel fast these days, with social media and twenty-four-hour news."

My mother persisted. "Do you have any clues, Maxwell?"

"Lots of clues. Can we change the subject?"

"I would guess it's a man doing these murders," she said.

Sandy attempted to rescue me with, "Mrs. G, you've got to give me the recipe for this bread."

"Although it could be a woman," my mother continued. "Or a Jack the Ripper type women hater."

My mother's interest in the murders arose from her concern for my safety, not the conclusion of the investigation. Like Marlene, she'd spent years worrying about me each time I'd left for work. A cop's mother feels the same anxieties as a cop's wife.

"We'll solve the case, Ma. The killings will stop. This is no different from any other case I've been on."

"Aunt Theresa is a nervous wreck."

"Stop believing what you see on TV," I said. "There is no serial killer loose. Where is Aunt Theresa, anyway?"

"She took the train to Connecticut to visit her son, Anthony." And then to Sandy, "Max's cousin. She said she feels safer away from the area."

"Well, tell her she has nothing to worry about. The both of you are safe here," I said.

My mother said, "I hope," and speared a meatball.

After I had sampled everything edible on the table, more than once, I cleared my plate and loosened my belt one notch. Sandy and I cleared the table while my mother started the coffee machine in the kitchen. While the coffee brewed, Sandy brought out a plate of anisette cookies and a box of cannoli.

There was no further discussion about the moonlight murders. The subjects moved from marriage to family history to social problems of the day. My mother was persistent in keeping up with the news. Her problem was, she believed most of what they reported. I tried to make her understand that most news agencies have their own agendas and slant their reporting. Often, erroneous news reporting made solving crimes more difficult for law enforcement.

Our visit ended after the sun had set. At the front door, Sandy gave my mother a gentle hug and said, "Thank you, Mrs. G. I had a wonderful time."

"You come to see me more often," my mother said. She turned to me and said, "Marlene phoned me last week. She and the girls are doing fine."

"I know," I said.

"How would you know? You haven't been to see the girls at all, this month."

When I offered a meager defense, she interrupted me with a chastising tone. "You should spend more time with your daughters."

My mother hadn't been in favor of my pursuing a police career. Even as I worked on earning my criminal justice degree, she was less than encouraging. She'd said being a police officer was a dangerous job not suited for someone who intends to marry and start a family.

My interest in crime began from reading as many *Hardy Boys Mysteries* as I could get my hands on as a teen. My mother unwittingly bolstered my interest in crime by buying me a Hardy Boys magazine each week. I became fascinated by the how and why of crime. Subsequently, when my mother saw the success I'd attained. She came around with a hug, a kiss, and a proud smile. As the years progressed, she became more comfortable and understanding of my profession and realized I was doing what made me happy. Nevertheless, she delighted in admonishing me when the occasion arose for not taking her advice.

"I'll see the girls on the weekend," I said. "I intend to spend the entire day with them."

"I'm sure Marlene and the girls feel safer when you're with them. Especially with these *Moonglow* murders happening."

I smiled and hugged her. "Moonlight," I said.

As I drove Sandy back to her apartment, I was thinking about something my mother had said. Sandy saw the concentration on my face and said, "You're thinking hard. What's on your mind?"

"My mother had unknowingly offered me a new detail about the case," I said. "A similarity in the murders exists that I hadn't considered."

Sandy said, "I'm waiting."

I said, "Jack the Ripper had killed women of the same social class."

"All prostitutes," Sandy said.

"The Moonlight murderer's victims are also of the same social class."

"You can hardly put prostitutes and escort women in the same class," Sandy said.

"Although they're of a different social behavior, someone with a deranged mind might regard them all as prostitutes."

"There is that misconception about escort services," Sandy said. "And a woman can hate another woman as much as a man can. Gender has no part in this equation."

Sandy and my mother were right.

CHAPTER 19

Briggs was reading off his laptop screen. He said, "Autopsy and forensics reports on the Quinlan case." He spoke without taking his eyes off the screen. "They found plenty of fingerprints around the place, but nothing identifiable."

"Probably all Samantha Quinlan's," Danny said. "She lived alone."

"What about the cigar?" I said.

Briggs read further down the screen. "Good news and bad news," he said. "The lab lifted a partial print from the cigar and a ton of DNA."

"What's the bad news?" Danny said.

"There was no print match in our system and DeMarco has no DNA in the system to compare it to."

"Then we can't put him at the crime scene," Danny said.

"Not unless we get a DNA sample from him and it matches," Briggs said.

"Can we bring him in for questioning?" Danny said.

"Based on what? We can't prove he was at Quinlan's apartment," Briggs said.

"His record verifies he's had a troubled past when it came to women," I said. "And he's recently had a problem with Quinlan. Her murder fit the timeline. That might give us enough probable cause to bring him in for interrogation. Maybe we can get a DNA sample from him.

Briggs closed his screen and swiveled his chair back to face us. "Let's keep this latest murder quiet," he said. "So far, the press hasn't gotten hold of it. I'll make sure it stays that way."

Briggs wanted to keep the fourth murder from the public for obvious reasons. I agreed with him. Although I saw no connection to helping solve the case, it would at least prevent an unnecessary panic in the city.

Danny said, "What about DeMarco?"

Briggs leaned back in his chair and thought for a moment. "We haven't had a break in this case yet," he said. "Bring in Mr. DeMarco."

Danny and I took a ride to DeMarco's yard in South Jersey. We didn't call ahead and arrived unannounced. Lumberjack's face appeared as he opened the door a few inches. When he saw us, he said, "Whatta you guys want? Mr. DeMarco don't wanna see you."

I said, "You're not as friendly as you were the first time we were here."

Danny said, "Tell DeMarco we want to see him."

"He ain't here."

"Lying to the police gets you in trouble," I said.

"I've been in trouble before. Get lost before ya get hurt!"

I hated to be threatened, almost as much as I hated being lied to.

Lumberjack opened the door wider, enough to show us he was holding a three-foot-long two-by-four in his right hand.

"What're you going to do with that, whittle toothpicks?" I said.

He didn't think that was funny. I could tell by the shade of red his face turned and how he curled his upper lip. The two-by-four went up quickly and was on its way down when Danny reached out and blocked it before it could part my hair *and* my head. Lumberjack tried to yank the wood from Danny's grasp. Danny held on to it with both hands, trying to wrench it from Lumberjack's grip. He was having a hard time of it because of Lumberjack's gorilla strength, so I made a move. I delivered a right punch and then a left to Lumberjack's gut. A billow of air burst from his throat like a blowout, but he didn't flinch. So I hit him again with a right to his jaw. That did the trick. He dropped the two by four. His legs buckled, and he melted to the floor. He lay there with his knees drawn up to his chest, moaning and holding his gut. I said to Danny. "You alright?"

Danny nodded. I let Lumberjack moan a few times before I said, "Now you can tell your boss we're here."

"He doesn't have to tell me anything." DeMarco's voice boomed as he walked out of the back room toward us. "What the hell's goin' on?" He reached down and struggled to bring Lumberjack to his feet. He walked him to a nearby sofa where Lumberjack flopped down and closed his beady eyes.

"What do you guys want?" DeMarco said.

"We'd like you to come to headquarters for questioning."

"You push your way into my office and attack my man and expect me to cooperate."

"Assault on a police officer is a felony in the state," I said. I pointed to the two-by-four on the floor. DeMarco looked down at it, then back at Lumberjack. He said, "Stupid move."

When he looked back at us, he said, "I answered all your questions the first time you were here. What is it you want now?"

"You've become a person of interest in our murder case," I said.

"What a bunch of crap. Am I under arrest?"

"No. We want to ask you some questions."

"Ask me here."

"We want you to come with us," Danny said.

"I don't have to go with you if I'm not under arrest," DeMarco said.

I took my cuffs off my belt and held them up for DeMarco to see. Chrome bracelets can change a person's mind. DeMarco took his cell phone from his pocket and punched in some numbers. "You guys are pushing it," he said. "I'm calling my lawyer."

When we arrived at the precinct, DeMarco's lawyer was waiting for him. He was tall and slender and wore a three-piece sharkskin suit the color of which matched his silver-gray hair. We went to an interrogation room. DeMarco and his lawyer sat at the table. Danny and I stood opposite them.

DeMarco said to his lawyer, "I think these guys are trying to railroad me."

His lawyer said, "Don't answer anything questions unless I say it's okay."

DeMarco said to me, "Okay. Whatta ya want to know?"

I said, "Did you have an ongoing relationship with Victoria Quinlan?"

"You don't have to answer that," DeMarco's lawyer said.

Danny said, "Yes he does."

DeMarco said, "Quinlan again. I already told you I rented her a few times. I never laid a hand on her."

"We don't believe you," Danny said.

Danny was trying to get DeMarco to say something to incriminate himself by riling him up. It was a tried-and-true interrogation method. *Good cop, bad cop.*

"We believe your relationship with her was more than just an escort," Danny said.

"Don't know what you're talking about," DeMarco said. He removed a cigar case from his pocket and slid out a Montecristo. "Can I smoke?" he said.

"No," Danny said. "But you can chew on it."

DeMarco removed the cellophane from the cigar and pushed it into the corner of his mouth. Danny stepped out of the room, brought back a paper cup, and slid it across the table.

DeMarco said, "What's that for?"

"Someplace to rest it," Danny said.

"Where were you yesterday between the hours of three and six p.m.?" I said.

DeMarco chewed on his cigar, then said, "In my office, working. I never leave before seven."

"Can you prove it?" I said.

"I was alone."

Danny said, "It doesn't look good for you."

"You got nothing on me," DeMarco said.

"Maybe we'll find something," Danny said.

"Did you use your desk phone or cell during that time?" I said.

"I don't remember."

"We'll check the records," I said.

"Be my guest," DeMarco said.

"Would you mind placing your hands on the table," I said, "and spreading your fingers?"

DeMarco looked at his lawyer. "What's this guy up to, Benny?"

His lawyer said, "Do it."

DeMarco put his cigar in the paper cup and placed his hands on the table. "My mother used to do this to me so she could check if I'd washed," he said.

I looked at DeMarco's fingernails. They were rough and calloused and needed work.

We needed to get DeMarco to leave his cigar behind, so I made up some unnecessary business to distract him. "Would you stand up and face the wall, please?"

"Is this necessary?" DeMarco's lawyer said.

Danny said, "Just do it."

DeMarco stood and faced the wall. When he did, I slid the cup with his cigar in it away from where he'd been sitting.

"Now turn around," I said. "Slowly."

DeMarco did what I'd asked.

"Put your arms out to your sides and hold them there."

Demarco scowled at my request but put his arms out.

DeMarco's lawyer said, "Detective, this folly has no merit. Do you intend to charge my client?"

I looked at Danny and said, "Do you need anything more, detective?"

"I think we've got all we need for now," Danny said

DeMarco was still standing with his arms in the air at his sides.

I said, "You can put your arms down now. You look like a 747."

He lowered his arms, annoyed and humiliated.

"Thanks for your co-operation," I said.

Danny said, "Don't leave town."

After they left, Danny took the cigar DeMarco had placed in the cup and put it into an evidence bag. We had gotten the DNA we hoped for.

Later that afternoon, I was able to get the coroner's autopsy report on Victoria Quinlan. As I'd expected, they confirmed the indentations I'd seen on her neck but couldn't identify their origin.

Chapter 20

Before the end of the day, I received several photos of the Ellison crime scene rope from Detective Reynolds. There was a full-length shot as I'd requested and a closeup of both ends. It was a light-colored polypropylene rope that looked new. The shot was of the rope laying on a table like a writhing snake. There were no creases or indents from previous knots. One end was smooth, with no telltale signs of a knot ever having been tied in it. The opposite end had been fashioned into a large knot, but not the hangman's noose one would expect. The close-up allowed me to see how it had been configured. I knew little about knots so I did some internet research. After looking at a dozen or more photos of knots, I could match and identify the Ellison knot as a simple "slip knot", also known as a "noose knot." A popular Navy knot but not limited to naval use. It would make sense that Ellison made the knot out of convenience rather than taking time to fashion a hangman's noose. But why wouldn't he have chosen a knot that would have stayed secured around the ceiling beam? The further I investigated, the more I was believing Ruth Ellison. Maybe her husband hadn't killed himself. I phoned Ruth Ellison and told her I had information concerning her husband. She was eager to see me, so I drove out to her Bay Ridge home that afternoon.

The Ellison home was a colonial style structure painted a soft blue with white shutters. There was a matching white picket fence across the front yard. The lawn was in urgent need of attention. A blue Mini Cooper sat in the driveway covered with leaves and pine needles, indicating it had been sitting idle for a while. The house sat on a quiet cul-de-sac lined with maple trees and dotted with colorful Rhododendrons. The serene setting juxtaposed the turmoil and heartache Ruth Ellison had endured over the sudden death of her husband. I hoped the peaceful setting at least brought her some solace. At the front door, I pressed the door button and waited. A door mat read. THE ELLISON'S. The words implied a family unit, which, of course, there was none. I felt a sense of genuine sadness for Ruth Ellison, not pity, but a sense of heartache for her having lost a loved one. She'd been living alone, without a husband or children, and facing the prospect of an uncertain future. I hoped the news I brought would provide her some comfort.

Ruth Ellison answered the door with a smile that appeared constrained. She was wearing jeans and a long-sleeved white cotton blouse. I smiled back at her, and said, "Thanks for seeing me on such short notice."

"I'm glad you're here," she said.

She closed the door behind us and led me into a cozy living room. The room was modestly furnished and offered a warm atmosphere. On a mantel over a stone fireplace stood a framed photograph of Mike Ellison in his Navy blues. Another of a younger Mike bare chested wearing jeans and a "Dixie Cup cap" stood beside it. A larger photograph mounted on the wall above the mantel was a two-shot of Mike and his new bride smiling cheek to cheek into the camera.

Ruth Ellison saw me looking at the photos, then said, "Happy days."

I wasn't sure how to react to that, so I offered a smile and said. "I have news you'll be glad to hear."

She offered me a seat on a sofa and sat beside me.

"I've looked into Mike's case as you asked," I said.

She chewed her upper lip in nervous anticipation.

"What I've uncovered so far leads me to believe there's a strong probability your husband did not take his own life."

Ruth Ellison squeezed her eyes shut and lowered her face to her hands. I placed a consolatory hand on her shoulder. When she looked up at me with wet eyes, I offered her my handkerchief. She dabbed her eyes and blew her nose in it. "Thank you," she said. "A weight has been lifted." When she handed my handkerchief back to me. I told her she could keep it.

I said, "I have nothing conclusive yet, but I think I can prove what you believed all along about Mike's death."

Her eyes welled again.

"I thought I was bringing you good news?" I said.

"It's wonderful news," she said. "I knew the truth would come out."

I said, "Don't cry again. That's my only handkerchief."

She smiled and sat up on the sofa. "What have you found out?" she said. There was optimism in her voice.

"Are you sure you want to hear the details?" I said. "They may be unpleasant."

"I've been living with the unpleasantness for three years," she said.

I told her of my suspicions concerning the knots that were used and the lack of a proper knot used on the ceiling beam.

"Mike was a sailor," she said. "He knew how to make knots and which ones worked best for a particular application."

I said, "They found no fingerprints at the crime scene. There were no prints on the chair found beside Mike's body. His prints would be on the chair if he placed it where it was found. Having found no prints leads to the assumption that Mike was wearing gloves, but there were no gloves found on Mike or at the scene. Mike would have no reason to wear gloves or wipe off his own fingerprints. Therefore, someone else might have worn gloves or taken the time to wipe off their prints."

"You mean, like whoever killed Mike and made it look like a suicide?"

I answered with an affirmative nod.

As she walked me to the front door, I said, "I'll keep you informed of my progress."

"Thank you," she said. "I pray we'll find the truth."

I smiled and said, "Prayer helps."

On my way back to Manhattan, my cell phone buzzed. It was Ashley Allan. She sounded distressed when she said, "Detective Graham, someone tried to break into my apartment last night."

"How do you know that?"

"I heard a strange sound that woke me. I'm terrified. Please come. I'll tell you everything."

I arrived at the Caledon Apartments thirty minutes later. A young woman security guard stopped me at the main entrance. She was wearing a brown and gold uniform with a shiny gold badge pinned to her right breast. The cap she wore was pushed forward into her black hair; the rim almost covered her eyebrows. She gave me a serious look and asked what my business was. I showed her my shield and said I was there to see Miss Allan. She checked a listing on the wall behind her and said, "6-A."

I said, "Have you been on duty all night?"

"Since midnight."

"Did you see anyone suspicious leave or enter the building?"

"No. It was a usual quiet night."

I thanked her and took an elevator up.

When I arrived at Ashley Allan's apartment, she was waiting for me with her door open. Before I said a word, she pointed to the door lock. I saw what was an obvious attempt to Jimmy the deadbolt. The surrounding paint had been scratched and chipped and someone had pried one side of the bolt away from the doorjamb.

"Someone tried to break in here for sure," I said. "What did the police say?"

When she offered no answer, I said, "Didn't you call the police?"

"I called you," she said.

"You should have called the police immediately."

"I was stiff with fear in my bed," she said. "I don't have a home phone and my cell was in the kitchen in my purse.

"What time did this happen?"

"My bedtable clock read 2:15. I laid in the darkness listening to every sound, every scrap, and bang. I could only wonder how long it would take someone to get inside. After the noise stopped, I lay awake for hours until I fell asleep."

I walked out to the corridor and gave it a quick look. Although it was well lit, there were no security cameras that I could see. There were six other apartment doors in the corridor and a stairwell at one end. I checked with the residents in the apartment next door to see if they'd heard anything unusual. I knocked on the door and waited. The inside security chain jangled, and the door opened about four inches. A woman's face appeared, looking wary. I held up my shield and said, "Sorry to disturb you. I'm investigating a possible break-in at Miss Allan's."

"My God," the woman said. "I told my husband I heard an odd noise last night."

"What time was that?"

"Two twenty-two, exactly. I know, because I checked my kitchen wall clock."

"What did you hear?"

"A low tapping and a scrapping sound. My husband claims he didn't hear it. But he sleeps like a dead man. When the tapping stopped, I waited almost a full minute before I opened the door. I was afraid *and* curious. My curiosity won out."

"It always does," I said.

"That's when I saw Miss Allen entering her apartment. I assumed she was returning home late."

"Did you see anyone else in the hall?"

"No, just Miss Allan."

"What did you do next?"

"Went back to bed and laid there for the rest of the night listening to my husband snore. I was too upset to sleep."

I thanked her for her information and was about to leave when she said, "Are we in danger? This building is supposed to be secure."

I said, "I wouldn't be too concerned. Just keep your door locked, as usual."

Back inside Ashley Allan's apartment, she followed me as I made a cursory check of the other rooms. I said, "After the noise stopped, did you check your apartment door?"

"I never left my room. After I locked my bedroom door, I shivered in my bed. Eventually, I fell asleep. When I awoke this morning, I checked the apartment. Then I phoned you."

"Your neighbor said she also heard a noise. When she looked out into the hallway, she said she saw you entering your apartment."

"She's mistaken," she said. "I was frozen under my bedcovers."

"Who do you think she might have seen at your door?"

"Whoever was trying to break in."

"She said she saw *you.*"

"Impossible."

"Then we can at least assume it was a woman that tried to break in."

"If you trust what she claims she saw."

"Why wouldn't I?"

"Mrs. Gallucci likes her wine."

CHAPTER 21

Ashley Allan followed me as I checked a second bedroom, the kitchen, and the bathroom. All were secure. "Doesn't look like anyone got in," I said. "Is anything missing?"

The fear and anxiety she'd experienced seemed near the surface and ready to boil over as I watched her body sway from side to side while I waited for her answer. Her eyes rolled up into their sockets and her legs collapsed under her. I caught her in my arms and carried her to the sofa. After putting a pillow under her head, I went to the kitchen and brought back a glass of cold water. She opened her eyes as I lifted her into a sitting position and touched the glass to her lips. "You'll be alright?" I said.

She looked around and asked what had happened.

"You fainted," I said.

She got up and walked to a mirror and recomposed herself. "I'm sorry," she said. "This has never happened to me before."

"Don't be sorry," I said. "Are you all right?"

She said, "I think so."

When she walked back to me I said, "I'll stay with you awhile to be sure you're feeling okay."

She said, "That's kind of you. I can make coffee if you'd like?"

Although she'd regained herself quickly, I wasn't comfortable leaving until I was sure she'd be okay, so I agreed to the coffee. I followed her into the kitchen and took a seat at a small table while she started the coffee machine.

"Why would someone want to break in here?" she said.

"It might have been a random attempt at home invasion," I said. "Criminals often choose what they think to be the most vulnerable."

"But I have nothing of value."

"A B&E person doesn't know that. This is a high-end apartment building. The assumption is, everyone living here is wealthy."

"Why did they choose my apartment?"

"The psychology of crime is complex," I said. "Maybe whoever it was liked the color of your door or your brass door knocker. Or that it's closer to the stairs than the others."

"You mean they liked the idea of having access to a quick getaway?"

"Exactly."

After tying a flowered apron around her waist, she brought two mugs to the table. When the coffee was ready, she filled the mugs. From a cupboard above the sink, she removed a box of cookies, arranged them on a dish, and set it on the table. She looked comfortable in the kitchen, with a natural flair for homemaking. I wondered if she had ever been married. I slid a cookie from the plate and bit into it. "These remind me of the cookies my mother made when I was a kid," I said.

She said, "I don't bake, but I'm hooked on goodies, especially cookies."

I got bold and said, "You seem to have a knack for homemaking. Have you ever been married?"

She dunked a cookie into her coffee and watched it soak up the liquid before she spoke. I saw the reticence on her face and hoped I hadn't stepped over a line.

"I was almost married once," she said. "It seems like an eternity ago."

"Sometimes things don't work out the way we'd planned," I said.

"He was in the military. We were engaged, but he was killed in a helicopter accident."

I said, "I'm sorry."

"He was my savior. The one that would take me away from home."

I bit my lip to keep from asking her questions that she might find too personal. My questions were answered when she said, "I'm an only child. When I was very young, my parents divorced. A year after the divorce, my father left me with my aunt and I haven't seen him since. I'm ashamed to say it, but I was glad to see him go." There was self-pity in her voice.

I pushed. "Was he abusive to you?"

She hesitated before she said, "At times."

"Sexually?"

Tears rolled out of her eyes, leaving tracks on her cheeks.

I felt like crap for upsetting her and apologized again.

She went to the sink and splashed water on her face, took a towel from a hook on the wall and patted her face dry. She turned to face me with an apologetic smile. "It's okay," she said. "I shouldn't have burdened you with my melancholic history."

"We all have sad stories," I said. "But we don't always have someone to tell them to."

She sat down again and sipped her coffee. I thought I'd change the subject to abate her discomfort. "How did you get your position with the Moonlight Ladies?" I said.

The question seemed to surprise her, but she offered an answer without hesitation. "Mr. Benning was advertising for a secretary. I had scraped enough money together to put in a year of secretarial school. I needed work, so I applied for the position. When I interviewed with Mr. Benning, he offered me the position. I considered myself fortunate and accepted."

"And you've been happy there since?"

"Until I overheard his phone conversation," she said. "Do you think this attempted break-in might have something to do with Mr. Benning? Maybe he found out I came to you about his phone conversation."

"Why would you think he'd try to break into your house?"

"Maybe to kill me."

I didn't think she truly believed that, so I let it go. I finished my coffee and stood up to leave. She said, "Would you like to take some cookies for the road?" A smile came back to her face, which made me feel better. She wrapped a bunch of cookies in a napkin and handed them to me. I thanked her and slipped them into my pocket.

On our way to the door, I said, "You'd better let the custodian know about your door lock."

"I will," she said.

She held the door open, looking vulnerable and violated. I said, "You'll be okay. You don't have to be afraid."

"I don't trust Mr. Benning," she said. "Whenever he looks at me, it seems like he's saying, 'I know what you did.'"

She leaned against me and pressed her face to my chest. She felt warm and soft against me, invoking memories of my daughters' who use to cuddle with me on our sofa after dinner.

"I'm terrified," she said. "With five women killed already, I don't want to become the next."

Despite any words of comfort I might have offered Ashley Allan. I left her as afraid and vulnerable as she had been before I arrived.

I took an elevator down to the main lobby and spoke to the security guard I had seen earlier. I flashed her my shield again and said, "Who was working this entrance last night between the hours of one and three a.m.?"

She said. "I was. My last midnight tour."

"Did you let anyone in or out of the building during that time slot?"

"No."

"You seem sure."

"I am. It was a quiet night. No one entered or exited."

"Is the building accessible from any other location on this floor?"

"Only fire exit doors, but they can only be opened from the inside."

"So, someone could leave by one of these doors but not enter."

"That's right."

"What about loading docks?"

"Overhead doors only, secured with padlocks."

"Are there guards at those locations?"

"Only during normal work hours. Anyone entering this building after hours would have to go through this location."

"Did you see anyone exit an elevator last night or walk through the lobby?"

"No. Except for the front desk clerk and myself, the place was like a graveyard."

She changed the subject and said, "You sure ask a lot of questions."

I said, "Curiosity is my weakness."

I thanked her, left the building, and headed for home.

Someone had tampered with Ashley Allan's door locks. How did they sneak into the building? It might have been someone already living in the building, or a night custodian. It could have been the nighttime clerk at the front desk. Or even the night security guard. Mrs. Gallucci said she'd seen Ashley Allan at her door and no one else. But eye witness testimony is often unreliable. The possibilities were myriad. The *who* was as important as the *why*. I thought about it some more while driving home.

Chapter 22

I rent an apartment on Bigelow Street in the township of Green Ridge, New Jersey. A small community nestled within the Watchung Mountains just north of Interstate 78. The apartment comprises a large living area, a kitchen, a bath, and a hallway leading to a single bedroom. I rent the second floor from Mrs. Jankowski, who owns the building. She had given me the rooms at a better-than-standard rate as a favor to my mother, whom she plays bingo with every Friday night at St. Michael's Church. After my divorce, Marlene and I sold our home of fifteen years, settled our debts, and split the remaining cash. She bought a house at the Jersey shore and settled in with our two daughters, Justine and Christie, while I took advantage of Mrs. Jankowski's generosity. My daughters were the love of my life and although Marlene got custody, I could see them whenever I wished. Marlene's only rule was "call first."

I had furnished my apartment according to my modest needs. Although, you won't see it in the pages of *Apartment Living Digest*. After I met Sandy, she added a few items she said would warm things up. Her contributions included several framed prints, a menagerie of ceramic figurines for the end tables and coffee table, two throw pillows for the sofa, and a potted plant. She assured me they would add ambiance to the rooms. Over my bed, she'd hung two framed color prints she claimed were copies of priceless originals, a Pollock and a Picasso. One looked like a ball of string that had come undone, the other resembled a blue alien creature. I told her I didn't need a blue monster looking down at me whenever I climbed into bed at night.

She said, "Don't be childish."

I said, "It might put a damper on our lovemaking."

She said. "We'll keep the lights off."

Sandy and I were at my kitchen table enjoying an assortment of doughnuts I had purchased from Dunkin'. She was munching a Strawberry Frosted while I worked on my usual Boston cream.

I said, "When you eat a doughnut, do you eat the hole or eat around it?"

She picked up a crumb from her plate and tossed it at me. "Clever, but not funny," she said. I laughed and refreshed her coffee from the carafe on the table between us.

Saturday morning had dawned bright, crisp, and cool. The heatwave hadn't returned, much to the delight of the entire northeast populace. Sandy and I had planned a weekend of outdoor activities. She looked great, in the soft rays of the morning sun streaming through the kitchen window. Her auburn hair fell in soft folds over the milky whiteness of her shoulders. I could count on her eyes sparkling whenever she smiled at me. I kept thinking; about how lucky we were to be together.

I was feeling amorous and about to express my feelings when my cellphone buzzed me out of my reverie. Caller ID told me it was Ruth Ellison.

I said, "Mrs. Ellison. How can I help you?"

"I found a note under my front door this morning when I went for my mail," she said. "It was a warning. A threat."

"What kind of threat?"

"I'll read it," she read. " '*Your husband killed himself. Stop investigating further or you'll wind up like him.*"

"Keep calm," I said. "You're in no immediate danger. Can I come by this afternoon?"

"Of course," she said.

"Keep the note in a safe place until I get there."

When I ended the call, Sandy said, "There goes our afternoon."

I said. "She's in deep distress. I'm the only person she can rely on."

"I understand," Sandy said. "Do you want me to come along?"

"Why not? We'll take the scenic route. Maybe the afternoon won't be a total loss."

We arrived at the Ellison home ninety minutes later. When I introduced Sandy, she said, "I'm sorry we have to meet under these circumstances."

Ruth Ellison thanked her and said, "I'm grateful Detective Graham is helping me. He's been the answer to my prayers."

She led us to a home office to the left of the entranceway, where she slid open the top drawer in a desk under the front window and handed me a white legal-sized envelope. There was no writing on it or a postmark.

"Has anyone handled this envelope beside you?"

"Only the one that delivered it," she said.

I removed a plastic evidence bag from my pocket and put the envelope inside. I slid the note from the envelope by one corner and read the same warning Ruth Ellison had read to me on the phone. The words were written in blue ink in a slanted cursive script. The paper was of heavy stock and tinted beige.

Sandy said, "Written by a man."

I said, "How would you know?"

"A ballpoint pen was used," she said. "The lines in the script are heavy and dark. If they'd been made by a woman's hand, which is inherently less muscular, there would have been less pressure applied. Therefore, the lines would be thinner and lighter."

"A plausible observation," I said. "We'll see what forensics tells us."

I brought the paper to my nose and gave it a good sniff. There was no fragrance. Sandy looked at me like I was crazy. "I'll explain later," I said.

"Is this something I should take seriously?" Ruth Ellison said.

"A criminal threat is a felony in this state," Sandy said. "And should be taken seriously."

I said, "Sandy is a defense attorney."

Ruth Ellison said. "A detective and a lawyer. You've got both sides covered."

"Does anyone know I'm looking into the case for you?"

"I haven't told anyone," she said. "Do you have any idea who might have sent it?"

"Someone with something to hide who doesn't want the police poking around," Sandy said.

"Am I in any danger?"

"Have you received any other threatening letters?" I said.

"I hope this is the last."

"What about phone calls or emails?" Sandy said.

"There's just that note," Ruth Ellison said.

I said, "Have you had any contact with Hayden Benning?"

"No. I haven't seen nor heard from Hayden since Mike's funeral."

I put the note in the evidence bag with the envelope and sealed it. "I'll give this to the lab and see what they find. Meanwhile, I don't think you're in any physical danger, but be vigilant. If you receive another note or if anything out of the ordinary makes you suspicious, call me."

"I will," she said. "Do you have any more information about Mike's death?"

"Only what I've already told you, but I'm convinced he didn't end his life. The question is, who did and why?"

We left Ruth Ellison with mixed feelings. She was concerned about the warning note but comforted by my willingness to help her.

The rest of the weekend turned out in our favor. Sandy and I had dinner at Brannigan's on Saturday night, then went back to my place to channel surf for a good movie.

I tried not to let the demands of my job interfere with my time spent with Sandy. One of the contributing factors to my divorce was that I had made that mistake during my marriage to Marlene. I wouldn't make that same mistake with Sandy.

A whipped dog is a wiser dog

On Sunday, we attended a beer festival in North Jersey. We sat under an enormous open air tent, which housed rows of tables and chairs and a small bandstand behind a makeshift wooden dancefloor. We listened to a local band and sampled free beer and ale from wooden kegs. Sandy spent a good amount of time trying to get me onto the dancefloor, but I resisted until I exceeded my usual aggregate of alcohol, then shamelessly stepped onto the dancefloor to "trip the light fantastic." Sandy spent the rest of the evening trying to get me *off* the dance floor.

After making enough of a fool of myself, Sandy drove the Chevy back to my apartment while I rested my head on the front seat back and rubbed my throbbing temples.

She said, "Does drinking free beer tastes better than beer you pay for?" She was offering me an example of my overindulgent foolhardiness.

I said, "I didn't want to spoil your good time."

She said, "You spoiled it for yourself. Did you learn your lesson?"

I said, "Is this a cross-examination, counselor?"

"You're already convicted," she said. "Now take your punishment."

I smiled, closed my eyes, and fell asleep.

Despite the condition I'd been in, I slept well through the night. Sandy insisted on spending the night at my place . . . *Maternal love.*

My head felt like a water balloon on Monday morning. After a warm shower and a warm kiss from Sandy, I was myself again. I put on a pair of khakis, my Sketcher casual shoes, and a short-sleeved collared shirt. It wasn't as hot as it had been.

In the kitchen, I turned on the coffee machine and filled it with water. I set the table with two mugs, a couple of plates, the necessary utensils, and a carton of creamer. The coffee machine gurgled and hissed while Sandy whipped up breakfast for us. She had scrambled eggs and toast. I downed three pancakes and two mugs of black coffee. I was ready for the day.

I drove Sandy to her apartment and then headed to work. On the way, I stopped at the forensics lab and dropped off the warning note Ruth Ellison had received. When I arrived at headquarters, I found an email on my laptop from the forensics lab with the results of the DNA test on the cigar we had found at the Victoria Quinlan crime scene. The finding corroborated my suspicions. I kept telling myself there are no coincidences in police work. How did George DeMarco's cigar brand get into Victoria Quinlan's ashtray?

I dug deeper into the players involved in my investigation. I had unlimited resources available but was restricted by the amount of personal info I could legally get on any suspect. It was time for me to pay a visit to "Greasy John."

Greasy was my conduit to the street, where a network of nameless voices and faces apply their ware from behind locked doors and dark alleys in the name of pleasure or greed. Pitiless denizens who prey on the hopeless, helpless, and infirmed for monetary gain or self-gratification without regard for human feelings. In the past, Greasy provided me with information that was crucial to my cases. He became an asset to me and also a friend.

I drove the Chevy to 8th Avenue near 34th Street, where Greasy ran his newsstand. Selling newspapers and magazines was less than a lucrative sideline for Greasy. He derived his real income from illegal betting. He'd accept a bet on almost anything that ran around a track on four legs or wheels at a higher than normal speed. After having served two years in prison for improprieties against the law, John Arden—which was his legal name—made his way back into society, dedicated to the proposition that he'd learned his lesson and wouldn't break the law again. But old habits die hard and his penchant for unlawful gambling soon overtook his declared intentions. Greasy knew I was mindful of his actual game. He also knew I could put him into an orange jumpsuit at any time. But his game was secure, so long as he remained my reliable pipeline to the street.

Before he retired, Greasy had been a short-order cook, flipping burgers and scrambling eggs over a hot skillet in local diners and restaurants throughout the city. But it wasn't his culinary skills that earned him his nickname. It was his complexion that glistened as if he were in an endless summer sweat. Most believed his years over a hot skillet caused his aberration. Greasy insisted it was genetic. We never talked much about it.

I parked across the street and dodged my way through traffic toward the newsstand. Greasy was behind his counter, untying a magazine bundle as I approached. When he saw me, he paused and wiped his face with a balled-up handkerchief he'd removed from behind his overall bib.

"Detective Max Graham," he said. "How long has it been?"

"Since Hector was a kitten," I said.

At 78, his thin frame was already bending forward at his waist. The short gray hairs protruding from the sides of his Scally cap and the tuft of hair on his chin contrasted with his dark skin. We both knew why I had come, but went through the usual preamble anyway.

I said, "How've you been, John?" Although those who knew him called him Greasy, I referred to him as John, which he preferred.

"I'm okay," he said. "Getting hot again, though." He reached down into an ice-filled cooler and brought up two bottles of spring water. He slid one across to me. I opened it and swallowed a mouthful while he guzzled his. He began sorting magazines while he waited for me to say what he knew I would. I had compiled a list of names of the key players in my investigation, hoping he could supply me with additional info that might be helpful. If there were something I needed to know, he would bring it to me. Occasionally, he'd turn up nothing relevant, but usually, I could count on him to come through for me. I never questioned his tactics or his sources.

I took another drink and watched Greasy separate magazines according to their topic. He placed them into three piles, shuffling with the speed and accuracy of a Las Vegas blackjack dealer. When he finished, he wiped his hand on the front of his overalls and with a big smile, said, "That's how it's done.,"

I said, "I'm impressed."

I took my list and a fifty-dollar bill from my pocket and slid them under a rock paperweight. "See what you can do with this," I said. "Friday okay?"

He glanced down at the list, and said, "Monday."

I nodded and walked away. As I did, He said, "Keep your head down."

I said, "Watch your back."

The exchange of words had become a litany between us, meaning, "Thanks."

Chapter 23

The detective bureau was quiet for a Friday afternoon, which afforded me a good time to think about my case. I loosened my tie and leaned back in my chair. As I did, I spotted Danny Nolan entering the bureau. He walked to my desk and handed me a manila folder.

"Forensics on the Ellison warning note," he said.

I removed the report from the envelope and read it. Forensics found nothing of value on the note, but they did lift several prints from the envelope. I handed the report to Danny. He read it and said, "That changes things."

"And leaves more unanswered questions."

Danny sat in my visitor's chair. He said, "Like who benefits from the deaths of the moonlight ladies?"

"And who wanted Mike Ellison dead, and why? And are the two crimes linked?"

"Those prints will start us in the right direction."

"If we find a match in our databank, we'll have our suspect," I said.

"You think Samantha Evers and her boyfriend's blackmail scheme had something more behind it than just monetary gain?"

I leaned back in my chair again and said, "Unanswered questions. Let's vet this Leon, what's his name, and see where he came from and where he's going."

"I'm on it," Danny said.

As Danny walked back to his desk, my phone rang. It was Lieutenant McCaffrey. I rarely looked forward to taking McCaffrey's calls. Most often, he was looking for a favor or offering me one that proved to be fruitless. I had worked the streets in uniform with McCaffrey for several years until he made rank and transferred to the 32nd precinct. At the time, he considered the advancement proceedings a personal rivalry between the two of us, regarding me as his only formidable contender. The only candidate who could take the top spot from him. I took no part in that mindset and let him continue with his folly. The proceedings were fair and graded on merit. Although he was awarded the promotion and transferred uptown, he continued to hold on to an unwarranted dislike for me. I harbored no ill feelings for McCaffrey, other than the baseless animosity he exhibited toward me whenever he was in my presence. He had a propensity toward arrogance, and, at times, could be the epitome of professional ineptitude. I think the responsibilities of rank were sometimes beyond his mental abilities. Making the wrong decision in this job could get somebody killed. There had been no love lost between us through the years. I tolerated him only for the sake of professional courtesy.

When I picked up my phone, McCaffrey said, "Graham, I'm calling to do you another favor."

"I don't need any more of your favors, McCaffrey," I said.

"You'll thank me tomorrow," he said.

"Okay. What can you do for me?"

"My men made an arrest you'll be interested in."

I waited, knowing there was more while McCaffrey took his time gloating over being one up on me.

"I'm holding a guy charged with atrocious assault. You might want to talk to him."

"Why?"

"He's connected to your moonlight case."

"In what way?"

"He's the former husband of Andriana Blanchet, one of your principals."

I remembered Blanchet telling me she had been married and divorced before meeting up with Hayden Benning and accepting his offer of employment with thc Moonlight Ladies. She hadn't mentioned the details of that marriage and I didn't ask. But maybe there was a connection here. I'd have to accept McCaffrey's offer and talk to this guy.

"When can I see him?" I said.

"He's being arraigned at ten o'clock tomorrow morning. If you get here before that, I'll make it happen."

"I'll be there by nine., I said.

McCaffrey said, "What, no thank you?"

He was rubbing it in.

I said, "See ya tomorrow," and hung up.

I arrived at the 32nd by eight the next morning. McCaffrey met me at his desk with a handshake and a phony smile. He looked like he had gained some weight since our last encounter, and his red hair was showing signs of gray. Although I accepted his hand, there were no cordial salutations between us.

I said, "What did this guy do to get himself arrested?"

"He beat up his live-in girlfriend," McCaffrey said. "Put her in a hospital. She's in a coma."

"What else should I know?" I said.

"I'll let you find out what you want from him." He picked up his desk phone, said a few words, then hung up. "Let go downstairs," he said.

We took an elevator to their lockup area in the basement. When the elevator doors opened, we walked down a windowless corridor, passing a uniformed officer who saluted McCaffrey.

McCaffrey didn't return the salute. *Arrogance.*

We entered a small interrogation room, which looked more like a reception area. There was a sectional sofa against one wall and a round table in the room's center. Only two folding chairs accompanied the table. An empty water cooler stood against the opposite wall. Above it, one barred window let in the grayness of the morning.

McCaffrey reached up and clicked on the interrogation light above the table. "They're bringing him down now," he said. "You want me to stay?"

"I can handle it," I said.

There was a knock on the door. When McCaffrey opened it, a uniformed officer appeared with a guy wearing jeans and a wrinkled long sleeved collared shirt. He looked like he had slept in them. His wrists were cuffed in front of him. His hair was tousled and the top three buttons of his shirt were undone. I took him to be in his mid-thirties, tall and built well. Dark areas under his eyes told me he had slept little.

"Take a seat," McCaffrey said.

The guy sat and placed his cuffed hands on the table.

"This is Detective Graham," McCaffrey said. "He wants to ask you some questions."

The guy didn't speak.

"I'll be outside if you need me," McCaffrey said.

After McCaffrey and the officer left, the guy said, "It's hot in here."

I clicked off the interrogation light above the table and flipped up the wall switch for the fluorescent ceiling light. I took a seat opposite him.

"Thanks for agreeing to see me," I said.

"I didn't agree," he said.

"What's your full name," I said, "for the record."

"Charles, no middle name, Blanchet."

"What do you do for a living, Charles?"

"I'm a truck mechanic."

"Can you tell me about your relationship with your former wife, Adrianna?"

"Why the interest in Adrianna?" he said. "I'm the one who got arrested."

"She's a person of interest in a murder case."

"Adrianna wouldn't murder anyone."

"She's a person of interest," I said. "How long were you married to her?"

"Three and a half years."

"Children?"

"No."

"Was it a good marriage?"

"Until she became involved with Benning."

"She was seeing Hayden Benning while you were married to her?"

He leaned forward and looked at me with an intense expression and said, "Yes. Do you know what that's like, detective? To find out the wife you love has been sleeping with another man?"

When I interviewed Adrianna Blanchet, she told me she'd been married and divorced before accepting work from Hayden Benning.

Another lie in her column.

I thought about my years with Marlene and couldn't envision her ever cheating on me. Although our marriage wasn't perfect, there had been a bond of loyalty between us, cemented by genuine love.

I said, "I'm not married."

"It's a violation," he said. "A feeling your whole life is changing in front of you and there's nothing you can do about it. First, there's disbelief, then disbelief smelts into sorrow. Then sorrow grows into anger, then hatred, and then rage. Rage directed at your wife and her lover."

"Do you feel rage for Benning or your ex-wife now?"

"I hate Benning for disrupting my life. But I forgave Adrianna after the divorce. She's not in love with Benning. She's in love with what Benning stands for."

"What do you mean?"

"Potential riches, Potential fame. Elevated status in life. Things I couldn't give her on a mechanic's salary. Adrianna believed she'd be on the threshold of obtaining these things if she hooked up with Benning. He was building a multi-million dollar business and Adrianna wanted to reap the benefits."

"Have you confronted Benning about the situation?"

"No."

"Do you hold any hostility toward him?"

"Sure. It was his business that took Adrianna away from me."

"Do you know Benning's business partner, Mike Ellison?"

"Never met him."

"Have you been in contact with Benning or your ex-wife?"

"No. There's nothing that can be done now, except hope his business collapses. Without his business, Benning would be nothing and Adrianna would lose the allure."

"So you'd be happy if Benning's business was destroyed?"

"It might bring Adrianna back to me—*revenge is sweet*."

"How'd you get into this mess with your former girlfriend?"

"It was an accident, but they're charging me, anyway."

"Have you been arrested before?

He hesitated.

"I can look it up," I said.

"Once before," he said, "for assaulting a fellow employee. Sometimes my temper gets away from me."

"Like it did the night you punched your girlfriend around?"

"I told you it was an accident."

"An accident *you* caused that put her in a coma. If she dies, the charge goes from assault to manslaughter."

I slid my chair back and stood up. "What would you do to Hayden Benning if you saw him today? Would that rage you talked about erupt? Would you want to destroy him for what he'd done to you?"

Blanchet sat back in his chair and said, "Detective, are you trying to link me to the murders of Benning's employees?"

"I'm investigating multiply murders," I said. "You have a viable motive."

"Do you think I'm your killer?"

"What I think doesn't matter," I said. "Only the evidence matters."

"Well, if you can prove I'm your *Jack the Ripper*, have at it."

***

Danny brought two cups of coffee with him and placed one on my desk. He sat in my visitor's chair and said, "There's motive there."

I said, "Maybe."

"More than maybe," he said. "As Blanchet said, if he destroys Benning's business, he destroys Benning. What better way to accomplish that than to instill fear in his employees by eliminating them one by one?"

"Eliminating them by killing them?" I said. "You're reaching."

"I don't think so," Danny said. "Snuff out a few and inevitably, no women would work for him. The adverse publicity would end his client list . . . goodbye Moonlight Ladies."

I took a drink of coffee. It was good. I said, "I guess you found a new barista."

"I did. The coffee machine in the visitor's lounge," he said.

I laughed and took another drink. "If Blanchet is willing to commit murder, why didn't he just kill Benning?" I said.

"Because he wants to punish him, make him suffer. Ruin his life like Benning ruined his."

I finished my coffee, put the lid back on the cup, and dropped it into my wastebasket. “I’m not sure Blanchet’s a murderer,” I said.

“And you can tell by the ten-minute talk you had with him? If he’s not a suspect, then your way of thinking brings us back to the same question. Who’s killing the Moonlight Ladies?”

CHAPTER 24

Based on what Charles Blanchet had told me, Danny's theory was plausible. There was a definite motive and a credible possibility. He had no criminal history other than two assault charges. During our conversation, he showed no remorse for what he'd done to his girlfriend. My perception told me this guy *wasn't* a murderer, but my cynicism told me *he was*. I trusted Danny's instincts and added Blanchet to my suspect list. He was a person of interest I couldn't ignore.

They arraigned Charles Blanchet the morning after I'd interviewed him and released him on five-thousand dollars bail pending his trial. If his girlfriend succumbed to her injuries, his bail would be revoked and they would arrest him on an upgraded charge of manslaughter.

I asked McCaffrey to send me everything he had of Blanchet's history. I received the info on my computer screen that morning, along with McCaffrey's snide remark: "Here's another one you owe me."

Charles (no middle name) Blanchet had been born in Chicago, Illinois, forty-two years ago. The first child of Judith and Charles Blanchet senior. A second child, (female) had been born two years later, (Whereabouts unknown). His childhood was stable and uneventful. He attended Road Line school in Chicago and learned to repair eighteen-wheelers. He found permanent work with a trucking company in Secaucus, New Jersey. Subsequently, he met Adrianna Evers. They dated and married. Their marriage was stable and survived just beyond three years until Adrianna become involved with Hayden

Benning. A divorce ensued, and the principals parted ways. Blanchet hooked up with a woman half his age who had been living with him in his rented apartment in Secaucus.

During the time after the divorce, he'd been arrested for beating up a sales agent. He paid a fine, and they dropped the charges. He had no other run-ins with the law until his recent arrest for thrashing his girlfriend. This guy had trouble controlling his temper. But was he a murderer? I intended to find out.

I wanted to interview Blanchet further, either to prove Danny right or mitigate my suspicion and shorten my suspect list. Based on Danny's theory, my suspicions, and the details of the circumstance, Judge Whitaker saw it as enough probable cause to sign off on a search warrant for Blanchet's apartment.

Danny and I rode to Secaucus early the next morning. We made the trip without prior notice. Charles Blanchet lived in a two-story garden apartment on Greenwich Street with Adrianna while they'd been married. After their divorce, he kept the apartment while Adrianna moved on to greener pastures.

I parked the Chevy across from Blanchet's building. We walked into the main entrance and climbed the stairs up to the second floor. The door to Blanchet's apartment was at the end of a carpeted hallway. Its walls were dull with an outdated motif. The area smelled of Jasmine and disinfectant cleaner. Danny wrinkled his nose and said, "I think the cleaning service is a bit overzealous."

I knocked on the door and waited. Behind the door, an orchestra played an up-tempo arrangement in a distant room. There was a lot of brass and percussion.

I said, "Benny Goodman."

Danny said, "Tommy Dorsey."

The door opened.

A young woman stared at us with a hard face. I took her to be in her late twenties. She was well dressed in designer jeans and a flowered cotton blouse. Her blonde hair was short and fashioned with bangs. She said, "Who are you?"

I held up my shield.

She said, "Is Charlie in trouble again?"

I said, "We'd like to talk to him."

"He's not here."

"When will he be back?"

"I don't know. He's out of town on business."

"He's not supposed to be out of town. He's released on bail with conditions."

"Are you going to arrest him?"

"No. We want to talk to him."

"I told you he's not here."

"Then we'll talk to you," Danny said.

"About what?"

"About him," I said.

"Do you have a warrant?"

"For what?" I said.

"To talk to me."

"No. But I've got one to search the premises if I need to."

I took the warrant from my pocket and held it up for her. She opened the door and said, "Come in."

She led us into an open living area furnished with lots of chrome, glass, and faux leather. The wall to wall carpet was worn in spots. There were live plants in ceramic pots, some as high as four feet. On one wall hung several large prints of rock stars. Window drapes that looked like they needed washing obstructed the view out to the main street. I smelled Jasmine, but without the disinfectant smell.

"I'm Charlie's sister, Nadine," she said. "Have a seat.

Danny and I sat on a tan faux leather sofa. As she walked across the room to turn off the music, I said to Danny, "Glenn Miller."

Danny said, "Dorsey."

I had to be right one of these times.

She came back and sat on a chair opposite us, crossed her legs and arms, and waited to hear what we had to say. Our presence annoyed her, and it showed in her demeanor.

I said, "It's my understanding your brother has been living with his girlfriend."

"I moved in here after the accident. Charlie doesn't like being alone."

"Are you married?" Danny said.

"I thought you came here to talk to my brother."

"Your history is germane to this case since you're his sister," Danny said.

She said, "My history is what?"

I said, "Important to us."

She said, "I don't see why I have to answer questions if it's Charlie you want to talk to."

"If you just answer a few simple questions, we'll be on our way," I said.

She thought about that, then said, "I'm not married. I live alone in an apartment in North Bergen. I never was married and after what I saw happen to my brother's marriage, I don't want to be."

Danny said, "How well do you know your brother's former wife?"

"Well enough to know what she is."

"What does that mean?" I said.

"She's a sinister woman who ruined my brother's life."

"Because of the divorce?"

"Because of what she did to him."

"You blame her?"

"Yes, and that Benning. I hate them both."

"Does Charlie hate them too?" I said.

"He says he forgave Adrianna. I believe him"

"Why?"

"Because he still loves her."

"Did he forgive Hayden Benning also?"

She paused to make sure she said the right thing. "You can't forgive somebody for taking your wife—and your life."

"Did your brother tell you that?"

"No. It's my opinion."

"How do you harbor all that anger and not act on it?"

I was pushing her.

"Whatever Charlie does to make his life better again is up to him. I'll do whatever I can to help him."

"Did you know Mr. Benning's business partner, Mr. Ellison?" Danny said.

"I've heard Charlie mention him, but I never met him."

"What did Charlie say about him?"

"If he's part of the business, he's part of the problem."

"What does that mean?"

"You'd have to ask Charlie."

"Your brother told me he would like to see Benning's business destroyed. Do you feel that way, too?" I said.

Her face turned ugly. She sat forward on her seat edge and said, "I'd like to see the two of them destroyed. Someone should take their lives away like they took Charlie's."

"That's a pretty bold statement," Danny said.

Her face softened as she realized the cruel words she'd just spoken. "You wanted to know what I feel. Now you know," she said. "I'd like you to leave now."

I took the warrant and dropped it on the coffee table between us. I said. "We need to search the rooms. This paper gives us the right."

"What are you looking for? Charlie's done nothing wrong. He's already in trouble."

Danny said, "Your brother's a person of interest in a murder case."

"You think Charlie killed somebody?"

I said, "He's a person of interest."

She leaned back in her chair and crossed her legs again. "Search," she said. "But don't wreck the place."

Danny and I put on our blue latex gloves, which were S.O.P. I said, "Tell your brother to contact me as soon as possible. If I don't hear from him by tomorrow afternoon, I'll have to report him as a bail jumper."

There were two bedrooms and a bath, and a home office off of the main room. Danny gave the bathroom a quick look, then went into the smaller bedroom. I began with the larger bedroom, which was Charlie Blanchet's. On the far wall was a huge four-post bed centered between two bedside tables. It was neatly made and piled thick with pillows and a comforter. An enormous wardrobe rested against the wall to my right. Opposite that sat a dresser beneath a pair of full-length mirrors. A single closet was in one corner of the room.

I started with the drawers in the bedside table but found nothing untoward. I looked under the bed and ran my arm between the mattress and the box spring. I turned over the garments in the dresser drawers but found nothing. The closet held two sets of work overalls, a pair of jeans, two pairs of work boots, and a pair of well-worn running shoes. When I opened several shoe boxes, I found shoes.

Danny came into the room carrying a single sheet of paper after I had finished my examination of the wardrobe. He handed me the sheet and said, "I found it between the mattress and the box spring."

I looked at the sheet and said, "Interesting. Let's see what our host has to say about this."

Nadine Blanchet was sitting in the same chair where we had left her. She looked annoyed.

I held up the sheet of paper for her to read. "Does this belong to you?"

She squinted at it and said, "I don't even know what it is."

"It's a list of current Moonlight Ladies' escort women."

When she reached for the paper, I pulled it away. "We don't want your prints on it if it's not yours," I said.

She gave the list a once over and said, "I don't know any of those women."

"Does your brother?" Danny said.

"How would I know? Where did you find it?"

"In the smaller bedroom, wedged between the mattress and box spring," Danny said.

"That used to be Adrianna's bedroom while my brother and she were going through their divorce. Maybe she put it there."

"Maybe you put it there," Danny said.

"Or your brother," I said.

"That's crazy," she said.

"Why would Adrianna hide it under her mattress?" I said.

"Why don't you ask her?"

"I will," I said.

"What's so important about a list of names, anyway?"

"It's important when the names with check marks beside them belong to women who have been murdered."

Chapter 25

I was at my desk the following afternoon, checking my notes and rearranging my interim reports to Chief Briggs when my desk phone rang. It was Adrianna Blanchet.

She said, "Detective Graham, I thought you'd like to know I received a call from my former husband, Charles."

I said, "Why would I want to know that?"

"Because he threatened me."

Adrianna Blanchet had no way of knowing I had added her former husband to my suspect list. Her call to me cast more suspicion on her than on her former husband.

"Did he threaten your life?"

"Not in so many words," she said.

"Then how and why did he threaten you?" I said.

"At first he was cordial, pretending he just wanted to hear my voice. I was cordial in return as we talked about old memories. But as the conversation continued, I felt his belligerence building. When I mentioned Hayden, he became hostile. He said he didn't want to hear about Hayden. That Hayden was the one that had ruined our life together. When I tried to quiet him, he turned his anger on me. 'You betrayed me,' he said. 'I gave you everything, and you left me for a high-class pimp! You should be punished along with him.'"

I didn't know what she expected me to do with the information. I was well aware of Charlie Blanchet's animosity toward Hayden Benning. It didn't surprise me to hear what he had said to Adrianna Blanchet.

"What would you like me to do?" I said.

"I'm afraid of him," she said. "Him and his crazy sister."

"Have either of them threatened you with physical harm?"

"No. But he sounded menacing enough. I think they've been involved with something."

"What are you saying?" I said,

"With what's been going on to hurt Hayden and the business, I mean, the murders, the fear instilled in the girls so they won't work. And the unfortunate death of Haden's partner."

"Mike Ellison took his own life," I said.

There was a brief silence before she said, "I have my doubts."

I said, "What do you mean?"

"What if Mike's death was the beginning of a plot to destroy Hayden? What if Mike didn't take his own life?"

"Official reports conclude it was suicide."

"What if there are more people involved than you think? Some people hold a deep animosity toward Hayden Benning. It's easy for a man of his stature to make enemies."

"Are you suggesting your former husband and his sister may have something to do with the death of Mike Ellison?"

"I'm saying I know Charlie's bad temper and how easily his anger erupts into violence. Evident by the recent beating he gave his girlfriend. I know the ill feelings he holds for Hayden, and I'm afraid for him . . . and me. I suggest you do some checking on them both."

"I understand your concern," I said. "But unless your ex-husband or his sister threatens you directly, there's nothing the law can do. The moonlight case is ongoing. If I find they're involved in any way, I'll pursue that avenue."

Arianna Blanchet's sudden apprehension for her ex-husband and his sister was puzzling to me. She hadn't told me anything about either of them during the two times I had interviewed her. Why the sudden concern? I offered her some words of comfort and ended the call.

As I put the receiver back onto its cradle, I realized someone was standing in front of my desk. When I looked up, Charles Blanchet was looking at me with a hard face.

"I got your message," he said.

"You broke your bail," I said.

"I had business to take care of."

"If you do it again, they'll arrest you."

"What did you want to see me about?"

I pointed to my visitor chair.

He sat.

I said, "I just got off the phone with your ex-wife."

He offered no response.

"She's afraid."

"Of what?"

"Of you. She said you verbally threatened her."

"Why would I do that?"

"You tell me."

"My problem is with Benning, not her. Besides, I haven't laid eyes on her for a long while."

"She said you phoned her yesterday."

"Not true."

"I can check her phone record."

"I've been out of town for two days," he said. "If I wanted to talk with her, I'd have called her before I left, or when I got back."

I said, "When we spoke with your sister. She expressed a lot of anger toward Benning and Adrianna. Her attitude doesn't put her in a good spot within this investigation."

"I'm the only family Nadine's got. She is fiercely loyal."

"Loyal enough to commit a crime?"

"We've been down this road, detective. If you're sure we committed a crime, then make an arrest."

"We found a paper with a list of names on it under the mattress in your ex-wife's bedroom."

"Nadine told me."

"Do you know how it got there?"

"I've never seen it."

I had gotten the list back from the forensics lab earlier that morning. I opened my top drawer and hand it to Blanchet. He scanned it from top to bottom. "This list means nothing to me," he said.

I said, "It means something to Adrianna. Her fingerprints are all over it."

He dropped the list onto my desk and said, "What does it prove?"

"Maybe nothing," I said, "But it puts Adrianna in a bad light."

I put the list back into my drawer and said, "Has your sister had any contact with Adrianna?"

"Why would she?"

"Did she know Mike Ellison?"

"No."

"How well did *you* know him?"

"I told you before, I never met him."

"But you knew who he was."

"Sure. He was Benning's business partner."

"Then you know he took his own life?"

"I heard."

I turned to my laptop screen and brought up my calendar. I said, "Your court date is in two weeks. Don't leave town again or it'll be sooner."

He stood and said, "Do you have any more questions you'd like to ask me or my sister? If you do, ask them now. I'm tired of answering questions about a crime I didn't commit. I'm not a part of your murder case.'

I said, "Your ex-wife seems to think differently."

CHAPTER 26

Our search of Charles Blanchet's residence produced nothing other than the list of murdered moonlight ladies. I couldn't connect the list to Charles Blanchet or his sister, but Adrianna Blanchet's fingerprints moved her up on my suspect list. Why would her prints alone be on the list, and why would she keep such a list?

I'd hoped to reduce my suspect list, but instead, lengthened it by adding Nadine Blanchet's name. She was a woman carrying enough hatred to want to harm Hayden Benning and Adrianna Blanchet, which made her a viable suspect. I intended to check her background and see what she's made of. After having spoken to Charlie Blanchet twice, I was still uncertain of his guilt or innocence.

I was heading home after a long day. The sun was setting behind a mountain range of light and dark clouds. The smell of rain hung heavy in the air. I was tired and looked forward to a quiet evening. The only company I wanted was a tv dinner, a six-pack of cold beer, and a good movie. As I turned off 34th Street for the Lincoln Tunnel entrance, my cell phone buzzed. It was Ruth Ellison. Her voice was a shaky whisper. "Detective Graham," she said, "someone has broken into my house."

I said, "When?"

She said, "Right now."

I pulled to the curb and said, "Did you phone the police?"

"You *are* the police," she said.

"Where are you?"

"Buried deep in my backyard shrubbery. "

"Are you hurt?"

"No. I slipped out my back door without being seen."

"Is someone in your house now?

"Yes. I can see him through my windows, walking around, searching for something. Come quick."

"Call your local police," I said. "They'll get there quicker."

"Hurry," she said and ended the call.

I knew it would take at least thirty minutes to get to Bay Ridge from my location. The right thing to do was to phone the Bay Ridge PD from my cellphone. Instead, I turned the Chevy around, got on the FDR, and headed for the Brooklyn Bridge. I figured Ruth Ellison felt more secure with me on the scene and I owed her that much. I didn't know who or what was inside her home or what their intention was. I hoped I was doing the right thing.

By the time I'd arrived at the Ellison home, it was almost dark. There were only subtle rays of light on the landscape. I parked a block away and walked toward the house, keeping in the shadows as much as I could. The neighborhood was quiet, other than the occasional echo of a barking dog. As I walked closer to the house, I wondered where Ruth Ellison was. She'd said she was hiding in a backyard shrub.

I stood in a shadow beside a utility pole and looked into the rear yard. There was no movement. A high hedge bordered the perimeter of the property. She could be anywhere within the tangled branches. I couldn't yell out to her, so I moved along the hedgerow, hoping she would spot me first. The house was dark except for the dim rays of daylight entering through the windows. There was no movement behind the windows. I darted across the sidewalk and moved across the lawn to a row of hedges. I moved along the hedge, trying to conceal myself, yet keeping myself visible enough to make Ruth Ellison aware of my presence. I looked up at the house. The silhouette of a man passed by a window. He appeared to be in no hurry.

I was about to move closer to the house when I heard Ruth Ellison whisper my name from a shrub to my right. I crouched low and went to her. She was on her knees concealed behind the branches of a huge rhododendron. She said. "What took you so long?"

I said, "Traffic was heavy. Has anything happened since you phoned me?"

"He's just been strolling around the house."

"Maybe he can't find his way out," I said. I was trying to lessen her concern; she didn't think that was funny.

I said, "How did he get in?"

"He broke the outer door lock. The inner door was shut but unlocked. When I heard the noise, I looked out the living room window and saw him working on the door lock. He took his time with the lock. I believe he thought the house was empty."

"Did you see what he looked like?"

"No. His head was down and he wore a knitted cap. I noticed his long hair hanging out the back of the cap. "

"Anything else you remember about him?"

"No. I hurried out the back door and called you."

"He knew you were in the house," I said. "He was giving you time to run."

"I don't understand," she said.

"I'll explain later."

I looked back at the house. There was no movement through the windows.

I said, "Do you have your cell phone?"

She held it up for me to see.

"My car is parked down the street. You can't miss it. It's the Chevy with the duct tape on it. Get in it, lock the doors and wait for me. If I'm not back in fifteen minutes, call the Bay Ridge police and tell them what's happening."

"Where're you going?"

"To see what this guy's up to."

"Is that a smart thing to do? Maybe I should call the police now."

"You should have called them before you called me," I said. "Go now."

I watched her dart across the lawn, down the sidewalk, and climb into the Chevy. I pressed myself against the rear of the house after crossing the lawn. I inched my way to the front porch and peered through a front window. Nothing was moving in the living room.

I kept my hand on my holstered gun as I moved toward the front door. The door was open a few inches, the lock hanging from its screws. I pushed the door back with my shoulder, opened the inside door, and stepped into the living room. The room was in heavy shadow. I tried to see as much as I could of the other rooms, but I could only make out gray forms and vague reflections. I made my way to the kitchen. The back door was open, left that way when Ruth Ellison made her hasty exit. I walked back through the living room toward the dining room. This part of the house was almost in total darkness.

As I passed through a hallway, my senses alerted me to movement in the shadow to my right. As I turned, something came down heavy on my head. Icy pain shot from my head and down my spine. My legs buckled under me and I hit the floor. When I tried to get to my feet, I was knocked to the floor again. I found myself in a whirlpool of darkness. Within the darkness, I heard heavy booted feet running through the dining room toward the rear of the house.

I struggled to my feet with the aid of a doorframe and took a few deep breaths while I waited for the merry-go-round to stop. I peered into the rear room when I was able to focus. A wall of windows allowed in the moonlight. There was no movement. I took my gun from its holster, released the safety, and stepped into the room. As I did, a figure burst through the rear door and headed into the backyard. I ran out the door and down the steps to see him disappear around to the front. I ran back into the house and out the front door. As I opened the door, I saw him vault over a wooden fence and run down the sidewalk. I started after him with my gun still in my hand. He was a half block ahead of me and moving away from me fast. I resorted to the running technique I had used when I ran track at college. The lessons were there, but the physical attributes needed to execute them weren't. I cursed the flabbiness around my waist and stopped running. I leaned against a utility pole and watched him turn a corner and melt into the darkness.

When I got back to the Chevy, Ruth Ellison was crouched low in the passenger's seat. I asked her to unlock the car door.

She sat up and looked around and said, "Is he gone?"

I said. "Yes. Unlock the door."

She stretched over and lifted the door lock.

When I got in, she said, "Who was that?"

I said, "I don't know."

"Why was he in my house?"

"I wasn't there for the reason he wanted you to think he was."

"What does that mean?"

"I think he was trying to scare you into stopping the investigation into Mike's death. "

"He did a good job," she said.

"He didn't intend to harm anyone. Just put a scare into you. Although, he gave me a rap on my head. When he ran into me, he panicked. I wasn't supposed to be there."

She reached over and probed her fingers through my hair. "I feel a lump," she said.

I said, "Ouch!"

"I'm sorry," she said.

I escorted Ruth Ellison back into her house and followed her through each room while she checked to see if anything had been taken.

"Nothing's missing," she said. "It doesn't look like he disturbed a thing. The only thing broken is the door lock."

"I'm sure you'll be okay," I said. "If it'll make you feel safer, I'll ask the local police to give special attention to your house."

"I don't think he'll be back," she said. Then, as an afterthought, she said, "Do you?"

"He won't be back," I said. "He accomplished what he was sent for."

"To scare the beans out of me," she said.

At the front door, I made a check of the inner lock. The deadbolt hadn't been tampered with and was intact. I said, "Keep this door bolted at all times."

She said, "Do you think he was the one who sent the letter?"

"I don't think so. Whoever sent that letter sent him."

"My God," she said. "What would he have done to me if I'd been trapped in the house with him?"

"You took a chance by calling me," I said. "Next time, call the police first."

She said, "Next time?"

Chapter 27

Six weeks had passed since I began my investigation. It had been moving along with satisfying results. I had loose ends yet to tie and a few questions still left unanswered, but I was confident I would solve the case before the end of the week . . . until I got the phone call.

When I answered my desk phone, a muffled voice said, "If you want to see Ruth Ellison again, drop the investigation into her husband's death. "

I said, "Who is this?"

The line went dead.

I couldn't tell if the voice belonged to a man or a woman. My first reaction was to dial Ruth Ellison's home. Ten unanswered rings affirmed to me; the threat was real. Someone was making good on the warning note they'd sent to Ruth Ellison.

I rushed into Briggs' office without knocking. He was at the water cooler. When he looked at me, I said, "I just received an anonymous call from someone who may have abducted Ruth Ellison. Her life might be in danger."

He crushed the cup he'd been drinking from and walked back to his desk. "Did they say as much?"

"They want me to stop investigating the death of her husband."

I told Briggs about the warning note Ruth Ellison had received and the intruder that had broken into her home.

"Is her husband's death tied to the moonlight murders?"

"It may be," I said.

"Did they call your cell or through our system?"

"Our system."

He picked up his phone and connected with the communications dept. They kept recorded records of every phone conversation coming into and going out of the building. In less than twenty minutes, Sergeant Becker came in with a small recorder. He placed it on Briggs' desk and pushed play. The voice I'd heard on my phone played back loud and clear.

Briggs said, "Is that all?"

I said, "That's enough. This woman's in danger."

Briggs said to Becker, "Have you traced the call?"

"They're working on it now."

Becker tucked the recorder under his arm and turned to leave when Briggs said, "See if you can identify the voice using your *thingamajig* equipment."

Becker said, "I'm on it." And left.

Briggs said, "I'll notify Bay Ridge PD and have them check out the Ellison home."

I opened the office door and said, "I'm going out there."

Before I closed the door behind me, Briggs shouted. "Keep me posted."

I snatched an Impala from the motor pool, and with the aid of lights and siren, made it to Bay Ridge in twenty minutes. There was a Bay Ridge squad car parked in front of the Ellison home when I got there. I parked behind it and walked up to the two uniformed officers standing by the front door. One was fidgeting with the door lock while the other wrote on a notepad. I identified myself and said, "Is anyone inside?"

The officer who'd been writing on the pad said, "It's empty."

"Any signs of forced entry?"

"No. The front door was unlocked."

"Any signs of a struggle?"

"None that we saw."

I said, "I need to go inside."

He said, "Help yourself."

Inside, the living room seemed undisturbed. Everything looked as it had on my last visit. Including the framed photographs of Mike Ellison on the mantel. Now he was smiling out at an empty room. I checked the downstairs rooms and went up to the main bedroom. I saw nothing that made me suspicious. It looked like the house hadn't been occupied in a while. Outside, the two officers were sitting in their patrol car. I leaned into the passenger side window and said, "Have you called for forensics?"

The officer who had been writing in his notepad was still writing. Without looking up, he said, "Is it necessary?"

I said, "This is a potential kidnapping, murder scene. Who's the commanding officer on this call?"

"Lieutenant Margolis, but he had to leave. He was needed elsewhere."

I said, "I suggest you contact him and have him send a team here."

The officer continued writing until I said "—now!"

I waited on the front steps for thirty minutes until the forensics team arrived. After the three-person team entered the house, Margolis pulled up in his police car and parked behind the Impala. I walked up to him as he was getting out.

Margolis was a tall, thin cop with brown curly hair. He looked to be in his forties. I showed him my shield and explained my connection to Ruth Ellison.

"Christ, you think somebody kidnapped her just to get you off the case?"

"Looks that way," I said.

"That never works."

"You know it and I know it," I said.

"Get me a photo and a description. I'll put out an APB."

"I'd prefer if you didn't," I said.

He looked surprised when he said, "It's SOP. How the hell are you gonna find her?"

"She's an integral part of my case," I said. "I have suspects and connections. I'd have more success following the leads I have."

"It's your party," Margolis said.

"Would you send me the forensics report as soon as possible?"

"As soon as I get it, you'll get it," he said.

I drove back to headquarters and went straight to Briggs' office to give him the update on what happened at the Ellison home. He was at his desk, reviewing my case report.

"Their forensic is going over the place now," I said.

I knew what was on Briggs' mind when I saw a scowl come over his face.

"You didn't tell me you were investigating Ellison's death? There's nothing in your reports about it."

I had to be careful how I explained things to Briggs. If I even remotely strayed from the truth, he would know it. He'd had years of interrogating people, and his instinct for identifying a lie was uncanny. I had always been intellectually honest with him and didn't want to compromise his trust in me.

I said, "I was trying to help Mrs. Ellison. Looking into a few things for her. She believes her husband was murdered. The coroner's report said it was suicide."

"Is his death tied into the moonlight case?"

"It may be."

"How long was Ellison partners with Benning?"

"Two years until his death."

He read more of the report, then looked up at me. I had seen that look before and knew what was coming.

"By unofficially helping this woman, you've put her in jeopardy."

I had no response.

"What you did was completely out of protocol."

"I was just trying to—"

He cut me short with, "What are you planning to do about it?"

"Wait for the forensics report. They may find something to start with."

Briggs' desk phone rang. He answered it. Listened for a minute. Thanked the caller, then hung up.

"The call to you was made on a throwaway cell phone— it's untraceable. They're still working on the caller's voice pattern."

I said, "Maybe we'll get lucky. All we can do now is wait and hope we hear from the caller again."

Briggs said. "You'd better hope we do. For Mrs. Ellison's sake—and yours."

Briggs wasn't happy that I hadn't informed him of my helping Ruth Ellison. Although my investigation was off the record and on my own time. He regarded it as a conflict of interest and discourtesy to his rank. There was nothing unethical about it. Over the years, I had involved myself in personal investing on a pro bono basis for strangers and friends who had asked for my assistance. I enjoyed the challenge and the satisfaction of being able to help. At times, I was successful. Sometimes, I wasn't.

If I could prove Ruth Ellison's husband's death was connected to the moonlight murders, it would clear me with Briggs. For now, I was helpless. All I could do was wait for a call back from her abductor.

CHAPTER 28

The call came two days later while I was at my desk. This time, it was through my cell. My screen showed an anonymous caller, but the voice was Ruth Ellison's.

"This is Ruth Ellison," she said. "I want you to stop the investigation into my husband's death."

"Where are you?" I said. "Are you hurt?"

"You have to stop immediately."

Although she was doing her best to sound convincing, I could hear the coerciveness in her tone.

"Are you being held? Who's doing this to you?"

The feeling of helplessness I'd been dealing with overtook my sense of logic and I began asking dumb questions I knew she couldn't answer. Of course, she was being held. Of course, she was being coerced into making the call. Of course, someone was listening to her every word.

"Please! Please do as I ask?" she pleaded.

I had no choice but to agree to her request. "If that's what you want," I said.

"It's what I want," she said. "I'm being—"

The line went dead.

The conversation was over. The call had served its purpose. Ruth Ellison's abductor had verified that I'd agreed to drop her case. He needed to hear it from me. I was sure I was dealing with an amateur. A pro would not have accepted my verbal agreement and would have insisted on further proof of my intention. My hope was he would release her unharmed.

I called Sergeant Becker and gave him the phone number to see if he could trace the call. He got back to me in less than five minutes. The call had been made from Ruth Ellison's cell phone and transmitted from a cell tower close to the New Jersey docks. *Further evidence of an amateur mistake.* Ruth Ellison was being held in that general area. An hour later, Becker phoned me with the exact GPS coordinates of the call. With the aid of Google Maps, it was determined Ruth Ellison was being held inside a shipping container at the Port Newark container terminal. We were able to pinpoint the exact container by its Bluebird logo and the number twenty-three painted on its side and top. The container was among a group of derelict containers that had out lived their usefulness and were waiting to be destroyed or refurbished. Finding it might present a small challenge but not an impossibility.

When I informed Chief Briggs of the findings, his idea was to assemble a squad of officers to search and close in on the target area. I suggested Detective Nolan would be all I needed to find Ruth Ellison and secure an arrest. Briggs scowled at the idea, insisting it was too dangerous.

"We don't know how many people are involved in this," he said.

"How many does it take?" I said. "I'm sure we're dealing with an amateur. With the element of surprise, we can get it done with a minimum amount of risk."

I was working on the idea that the person who sent the intruder to Ruth Ellison's home paid that same person to make the abduction.

"How can you be sure you're dealing with an amateur?" Briggs said.

"Instinct," I said.

Briggs had bet on my instinct in the past and had won. He was betting on it again when he gave me the go ahead.

An hour later, Danny and I were in a Crown Vic, heading south on I-95 toward Port Newark. At the main entrance gate, we showed our shields to the guards and were allowed entry without question. The terminal is always busy. We followed a short winding road close to the water and continued out of the work area until we reached the section where they kept the empty containers. There were rows of them, some stacked three tiers high, and some lined up end to end in a single row on the ground. I drove to the section where they kept the single row of boxes.

Danny said, "There're hundreds of them in every color. And their numbers aren't sequential."

"Just look for a big white number twenty-three," I said, "and that Bluebird logo."

The air temperature that morning had been a comfortable seventy-eight. I couldn't imagine what the temperature would be inside one of those containers. Time was a factor in finding Ruth Ellison. If it wasn't already too late.

I drove at a slow, steady pace as we checked the numbers on each container on either side of us. There were single digits and double digits and multiple digits in no particular order. There were white numbers on black boxes and black numbers on white boxes and brightly colored boxes without numbers. Some boxes had logos, and some didn't. We hadn't yet seen the number twenty-three where Ruth Ellison was being held.

I made a right turn and drove down a second avenue between rows of boxes. We saw no number twenty-three. I took a left turn by the waterfront and followed it to a single row of boxes set close to the water's edge.

"There it is," Danny said.

The four-foot-high white number twenty-three glared in the morning sun directly in front of us like a city billboard. The Bluebird logo was beside it. We'd found the right container.

I pulled to the side of the road about a hundred feet before it and killed the Crown Vic's engine. Ruth Ellison was inside that hot box, hopefully still alive. I reached under the driver's seat and removed the bolt cutter we had brought with us. There were no words between Danny and me as we got out. We knew what we had to do.

We took out our weapons and held them at the ready as we made our way along the front of the boxes until we reached number twenty-three. There was a huge sliding door in the center of the box. It had been bolted with a chain and padlock as we had expected. There were no other doors or windows. The box was set on a steel platform several feet above the ground. The only access to the inside was to cut the chain and slide the door open. The element of surprise and the sudden burst of sunlight exploding in the darkness were the only advantages we had. If there were bad guys inside, they'd be caught off guard and blinded by the light at the same time. It was a strategy we hoped would work, but couldn't count on. We climbed up onto the platform and inched our way toward the door. I put my ear against the corrugated metal of the box, but it was impossible to hear any sound from inside because of the rumble of truck engines and cranes operating in the distance. Danny moved to the other side of the door from where I was. He took hold of the door latch and waited while I worked the bolt cutter on the chain. After the chain cut through, he was to pull as I pushed, sliding the door open as quickly as possible. At that point. It was anybody's game.

I slid a chain link between the cutter blades and gave it all I had. The blades cut through a coating of rust, showing bright metal beneath it, but were nowhere near cutting through the thick link. After taking a deep breath, I squeezed the cutter's arms again. Danny grabbed onto one arm of the cutter while I held the other. We squeezed the blades against the link. My arms ached and quivered at the amount of pressure I was applying. Danny's face reddened and morphed into a twisted mass of pain and exertion. I was about to give up when the link snapped. We pushed the door back on its rollers, washing the interior of the box with sunlight. We rolled on our backs onto the interior floor on either side of the opened door. I got up on one knee and scanned the interior. I saw barren walls and dark corners where the incoming light hadn't touched.

Danny was moving along the front wall toward a rear corner. As I started toward him, he dropped to a knee and pointed his gun into a shadow filled area. I stood back in the darkness and waited. When he holstered his gun, he looked back at me and said, "It's okay."

When I walked into the shadows Danny was on his knees, undoing the duct tape from Ruth Ellison's wrists and ankles. Someone had propped her up in a corner like a sack of grain. Beside her on the floor was a porcelain plate with the remnants of what might have been a meal. A clear gallon jug of water and an empty glass was beside it. The ordeal she'd been through was evident on her face. I kneeled beside her and pulled a length of tape away from her mouth. "It's okay now," I said. "It's all over."

A cursory check told me she had not been physically abused.

She widened her eyes as if she had just woken up. She looked disoriented and confused. I said, "Do you know me?"

She tipped her head to the left, focused her eyes on my face and smiled, then her eyes flooded with tears. I gave her my handkerchief. She wiped her eyes, then used it to wipe the sweat from her face and forehead. Her blouse was clinging to her arms and torso. The temperature inside the box felt like a hundred. I poured some water into the glass. It was warm but wet. I brought it to her lips and said, "Sip it easy."

She did.

"Can you stand?" Danny said.

She looked down at her legs and said, "I think so."

We lifted her to her feet and waited while she stabilized. She was still in a stupor when she said, "I don't know what they wanted."

Danny used his cell to call for transportation to the nearest hospital.

"I don't need a doctor," she said. "I'm okay."

"We'll let the doctors determine that," I said.

We walked her to the open door where the air was cooler. We sat on the edge of the box looking at the water.

"Where are we?" Ruth Ellison said.

"The banks of the Hudson," I said.

She said, "I don't know what he wanted. He wouldn't tell me what they wanted. He didn't talk. He never talked."

"Who never talked?" Danny said.

"The man who grabbed me from my yard. He put a hood over my head. I screamed in panic as he dragged me to a waiting car. The man put sticky tape around my wrists after pushing me into the back seat. I heard a man and woman talking in the front seat while we drove."

"There were three people in the car with you?" I said.

"I'm sure of it," she said.

"Did you recognize their voices?"

"I had a hood over my head. Their voices weren't distinct, but I'm sure it was a man and a woman."

I was thankful for the breeze coming in off the Hudson. The fresh air would help Ruth Ellison regain herself.

She said, "I could use a double cheeseburger and a Coke."

I said, "That's a good sign."

As the words left my lips, I heard a crunching of footfalls on the gravel to my right. When I looked, I saw a guy walking toward us. He wore wrinkled jeans and a sweatshirt and carried a paper bag stuffed with food items, and a bottle of soda. His black hair hung like spaghetti to his thin shoulders, partially hiding his pocked and unshaven face. Danny and Ruth Ellison saw him too. He walked close to the container wall until he spotted us. When he did, he let the bag and bottle fall to the ground, turned and bolted away from us, running along the row of containers. He had been caught, and it was time for him to run. I jumped down from the edge of the box and sprinted after him. When he turned into a narrow space between two containers, I was within twenty feet of him. I came out on the other side with him and watched him make a quick right. He was running hard. His legs were longer than mine and he appeared much younger. But I had my technique from my track running days at college to rely on. *I hoped.*

At the end of a row of boxes, he climbed onto a pile of fifty-five-gallon drums. He kicked a few of them down in my direction. They rolled and clattered in front of me, but I avoided them without breaking my stride. He wasn't used to running and was having a hard time with it. I could hear his labored breathing even as far back from him as I was.

He ran onto an open expanse or roadway where there were no containers. I took a couple of deep breaths and pushed myself harder. He was slowing down but not giving up. When I was close enough, I lunged for his legs and brought him down. We fell forward onto the ground. I got to my feet quickly and turned him to face me, expecting a confrontation, but he raised his hands above his head. I brought him to his feet. He let me cuff him like he was glad it was over.

As I walked him back to where I'd left Danny and Ruth Ellison, I said. "What're you running from?"

He said, "You."

CHAPTER 29

When I got back to the container, Danny and Ruth Ellison were waiting for me. Danny said, "Are you alright?"

I answered with a nod and said to Ruth Ellison. "Do you recognize this guy?"

She tapped the top of her head and said, "A hood, remember?"

She leaned closer to him and took a quick sniff. "He's the one who brought me food. He never said a word to me, but I smelled pipe tobacco whenever he came near me. I recognize the smell."

I reached into the front pocket of his sweatshirt and found an old Briar pipe; a pouch of tobacco and a Bic lighter.

"Is what she's saying true?" I said.

The guy didn't answer.

Ruth Ellison said, "He won't talk. He never does."

An EMT vehicle pulled up along with a port authority police car. We identified ourselves to Sergeant Nardone and explained the situation. Ruth Ellison refused to be taken to a nearby medical facility for a check-up, but she agreed to let the EMTs perform a preliminary on the spot, understanding that she'd have her primary physician check her out sometime soon.

We searched our runner for ID but he had none. Other than his pipe and his tobacco pouch, his pockets were empty. The paper bag he carried contained two cups of fruit yogurt, a soggy burger, fries, and a box of gingersnaps cookies. We put him into the back seat of the Crown Vic and waited for the EMTs to finish with Ruth Ellison. After they'd given her a preliminary okay, we got into the Crown Vic and headed for Bay Ridge to bring her home. She sat up front with Danny, while I sat in the rear seat with our runner. On our way. I tried to get him to talk.

"Do you understand you're implicated in a kidnapping?" I said.

He looked out the side window at the passing scenery as if I weren't talking to him.

I continued: "If you don't explain to us why you were there, you could be charged. Abduction is a serious crime. It carries a long jail sentence."

He took a deep breath and continued to ignore me.

"It's not like you were taking an innocent walk. I caught you red-handed heading for the number twenty-three box where Mrs. Ellison was tied up."

No response.

"And that you ran doesn't help you."

He remained steadfast and silent. I tried a different approach.

"If you co-operate with us, it can make things easier for you."

Without looking away, he said, "I didn't hurt no one."

"You hurt someone emotionally when you force them to do something against their will."

He looked at me for the first time when he spoke. "I helped her. I brought her food."

"Why?"

Another hesitation, then . . . "They told me to."

"Who told you to?"

He turned his face back to the window again and didn't answer. I could see his mind was reeling. He looked confused and even frightened. By his demeanor and speech, it was evident this poor guy had mental issues. He seemed harmless, even childlike, but sometimes harmless can be dangerous.

We drove for a few more miles before I said, "If you give me the name of who told you to do this thing, I might convince the district attorney to go easy on you. Do you know what a district attorney is?"

He shook his head.

"It's the person who can put you in jail for a long time."

He perked up when he said, "I don't wanna to go to jail."

"You might not have to if you give me a name."

He looked out the window again. He was thinking hard. I wasn't sure how much he could comprehend, but I hoped for his sake he understood what I was saying.

He sat quietly for most of the ride. When we crossed the GW Bridge, he turned to me and said, "If I give you a name, will you help me *not* go to jail?"

I said, "Scout's honor."

He thought for a moment, then said, "Okay, I'll give you a name."

***

We questioned our runner again back at headquarters. He gave his name as, John Carter Kagan. We identified him as one of New York City's fifty thousand homeless living in a shelter in the Bronx. The information he provided was enough to present to the district attorney to prefer a charge of kidnapping against those involved. The kidnappers had selected him to do their dirty work under a false promise of earning a great deal of money for a few days' work. He was being held until he could be mentally evaluated. Judge Whitaker ordered the evaluation based on Kagan's mental demeanor. If the court deemed him fit, his testimony would put the kidnappers away for a long time.

I had spoken with Assistant District Attorney, Marsha Alinsky, to let her know John Kagan had co-operated with us, and any consideration would be appreciated.

Armed with the identities of the kidnappers and the work I'd completed on the Moonlight murders case; I was ready to name names and make arrests.

Chapter 30

Saturday morning arrived before I knew it. I had promised Marlene (and my mother) I would spend the day with my daughters. It had been almost a month since my last visit and I felt guilty. I was happy to get away for a while. The moonlight ladies' case had dragged on and I was satisfied I had collected enough evidence to prove who the moonlight murderer was, and who had murdered Mike Ellison. On Monday, I'd submit my completed report to Chief Briggs and close the case. It would make him smile.

Until then, the moonlight ladies belonged to another world.

I was up by seven, showered, shaved, and ate a quick breakfast. I phoned Sandy and suggested we have dinner together at Branigan's when I got back from the shore.

She said, "Sounds great, but afterward, we'll have to find some indoor recreation to work off the dinner."

I said, "carnal or cerebral?"

She said, "strictly carnal."

I said, "I'm sure we'll think of something."

I blew her a kiss on the phone and ended the call.

I was on the road by 9 a.m. Saturdays are never a good time to drive the Garden State Parkway. Traffic was almost always bumper to bumper. But today the traffic was lighter than I'd expected. Maybe it was the early morning hour. I could cruise at a steady sixty-five without interruption. On the open road, my Chevy Nova rode like a Cadillac.

Meola Beach is a community on the Jersey shore south of Asbury Park. It comprises condos and bungalows and boasts one of the best beaches in the state. Marlene had always been a water person and used her share of the profit from the sale of our home to purchase the small house close to the ocean. I had never been a beach person. All that sand and wind gave me an itchy, gritty feeling. But seeing my daughters was a greater reward than any inconvenience I might have had to endure.

I made it to Meola Beach in just over an hour. I pulled into the gravel driveway and parked behind Marlene's Audie. The previous owner had painted the one-story house white. It still looked clean and crisp despite the salt air. A white picket fence surrounded the front lawn area, which had been covered with white river stone rather than green grass, an application ubiquitous to the locale. A brick walkway wound its way up to the front door, where a brightly painted windmill/mailbox hung next to the doorbell. Christie and I had built the mailbox as a brownie project. She had removed it from our former home and proudly displayed it in their new home for all to see.

I got out of the car and walked to the door. I was about to press the doorbell when the door opened to the excited voices of my daughters.

"Daddy's here!" Christie shouted.

"We knew you were coming," Justine said. She jumped up, put her arms around my shoulders, and held on. Christie wrapped herself around my leg and squeezed.

"Wow! What a greeting," I said.

Justine jumped down, took my hand, and pulled me through the doorway while Christie enjoyed a free ride in on my leg. I kicked the door closed behind me with my free leg as the girls guided me to the living room sofa.

Justine's hair had turned as red as her mother's, accentuating the roadmap of freckles on her cheeks and nose. She wore a blue sweatsuit and pink sneakers. Marlene had fashioned her hair into a ponytail and tied it with a matching pink ribbon. Christie still had that tomboy nature. The sweatsuit she wore matched her sister's, but her dark hair was too short for a ponytail.

Marlene had always had a talent for interior decorating. The living room was large but cozy with the contemporary motif she'd preferred. A two-seater sofa rested against the wall opposite the full sofa, bordered by two cherry wood end tables. In a far corner stood a glass cabinet displaying Marlene's ceramic dog collection. A large screen TV took up the remaining wall space. Window draperies corresponded with the fabric color of the sofa. The kitchen had been updated with Oak cabinets and stainless steel appliances. Through the opened doors, I could see into the girl's bedrooms. Marlene had transformed each into a wonderland of all the delights young girls love.

Marlene came out of the kitchen to greet me, drying her hands on a towel. She said, "How are you, Max?"

I said, "I'm okay. How are things here?"

She said, "Better, now that you're here with the girls."

Marlene looked good, despite what she'd gone through with our divorce. She still had an outstanding figure and although her hair had lost some of its sheen, it was fashioned as I remembered her always wearing it. She sat on the two-seater opposite me.

Justine said, "We have a surprise, Daddy."

Christie said, "Wait here."

Marlene smiled. She knew what was coming.

My daughter walked into Justine's room and a moment later came out carrying a ball of gray fur. "Look, Daddy," Christine said, "it's Floppy. See how big he's gotten."

Floppy sprang from Justine's arms onto the sofa beside me. In four short months, the kitten had morphed into an oversized cat. I reached out and scratch its head. It squeezed its eyes shut and purred in ecstasy.

"Floppy likes you, Daddy," Christie said.

When Floppy decided its independence had been infringed upon long enough, he jumped off the sofa and scurried across the floor into Justine's bedroom. The girls ran after him.

I said to Marlene, "I think you're feeding him too much."

She said, "The girls take turns. Sometimes they overdo it."

She stood up and said, "Speaking of food, I have the grill warming in the backyard. The girls want burgers and fries."

I said, "Sounds great. Can I help with anything?"

"Take the girls outside," she said. "I'll bring out what we need."

The backyard was of adequate size surrounded by a chain-link fence. A huge weeping willow tree stood in one corner, its low reaching limps hovering over the fence line and providing shade over the girl's swing set. The small patio close to the house was constructed of brick pavers and bordered with small boxwood shrubs. I had purchased a round outdoor table with an umbrella and four chairs that first summer Marlene and the girls moved into the house. A gas-fired grill completed my contribution.

Marlene brought out the food and accouterments for us to enjoy an afternoon barbecue. I helped her set the table while the girls played on the back lawn with Floppy. While Marlene saw to the cooking, I kicked the ball around with the girls and pushed them on their swings. "Higher, Daddy! Higher!" was the repetitive cry from Christie until she said she felt nauseous and asked me to stop.

The remainder of the day was enjoyable. Marlene was cordial but cautious, which had been her demeanor toward me since our divorce. I was my usual, affable self. We kept our conversation on family matters. Being careful not to break the unwritten rule we'd established after the divorce of not talking about my job. It had become an uncomfortable subject for us both, having been the prime reason for our breakup.

Marlene made sounds like a dinner bell and we all sat at the table and stuffed ourselves with hotdogs and burgers and washed them down with juice or soda, (no beer). After we ate. I helped Marlene collect the dishes from the table. She said. "I spoke with your mother last week. She said she's doing well."

"She is," I said. "Well enough to give me Hell for not seeing the girls often enough."

"It wouldn't hurt if you came more often," she said.

I fought back the urge to say, "*The job*", but she'd heard that excuse many times during our marriage and it had lost its credibility.

Marlene asked the girls to take the cat into the house to give him lunch. "And don't forget to give him fresh water," she said as they disappeared through the back door. When they were gone, she slumped down in her chair and exhaled a deep breath. She looked content but tired. I wondered if living alone and raising the girls had been putting an undue burden on her. I made a note to myself to become more involved in my daughter's daily activities and relieve Marlene of some responsibilities of being a single mother.

Maybe if I'd had that mindset during our marriage, we'd still be together.

We sat in silence for a full minute, listening to the easy wind through the willow limbs, enjoying the fragrant air, and the symphony of birds above us. Our eyes met when we looked across the table. It seemed like we were trying to communicate without words. Words we should have said to each other a long time ago. I wanted to say, *Maybe we can start over. Nurture whatever love there is still between us. Make it work, this time.* But the improbability of it ever happening made me feel silly.

My love for Sandy was fresh and genuine, with optimism for the future. The love I held for Marlene had been built on sharing togetherness and years of good memories. That kind of love can never leave one's heart, regardless of time or circumstance.

Getting back with Marlene was a fantasy I knew would never happen.

Marlene got up and began to clear the table. She said, "Your mother seemed very concerned about this case you're working on."

It surprised me she had even brought it up, but I guess my mother's concerns took precedence over our unwritten rule.

"She's being the mother of a cop," I said. "There's nothing to worry about."

I had made that statement to Marlene many times during our marriage. It *also* had lost its credibility.

Marlene said, "You mean like being the wife of a cop?"

That was a zinger I should have been ready for.

She said, "Have you at least offered her some words of comfort?"

I said, "Of course. But she believes everything she sees on the news."

"About it being a serial killer?"

I said, "Marlene, we've solved the case. It's closed. Soon, I'll submit my final report to my bureau chief."

"I haven't seen anything more about it in the news."

"That's because we've kept any additional information from the press."

"You know who the killer is?"

She gave me an inquisitive look, as if to say, *You can tell me.*

I said, "Don't ask."

Back inside the living room, Marlene updated me on the girl's progress in school. Christie had gotten the lead in the school play and Justine was advancing well in her violin lessons.

"Will you come to see me in my play, Daddy?" Christie said.

"Front-row seat," I said.

Marlene gave me a look that said, *"Don't promise if you can't make it."*

I looked back at her and said, "I'll be there."

While Marlene finished up in the kitchen, I played a video game with the girls on the large-screen TV. I enjoyed myself even though I had no idea what I was doing. Hearing my daughters tease and giggle made me enjoy myself even more. We laughed at my ineptitude and even Marlene joined in for a game.

After hugs and kisses from the girls and a civil, "Take care," from Marlene. I was on the parkway heading north. Traffic was bumper to bumper. I slid a CD into the player, expecting a long ride. I listened to *Doo Wop '60s* as the Chevy inched its way back to Green Ridge.

I was glad Marlene had purchased the house in Meola Beach. The town and surrounding area were clean, wholesome places to live. I took comfort in knowing she and the girls were safe.

Chapter 31

Chief Briggs got the phone call at 9:27 on Monday morning. By 9:28, I was in his office.

"New Jersey State Police have our man, Ramos, cornered in a warehouse," Briggs said.

"Cornered how?" I said.

"A local uniform spotted him getting off a bus. He recognized him from our APB. When they attempted to arrest him, there was a scuffle. He snatched an officer's service weapon and made a run for it."

This guy's getting more stupid every day, I thought.

"They followed him to an industrial complex where he ran into an abandoned warehouse."

"What's the situation now?" I said.

"They've got the place surrounded. He's throwing shots out a window at the police."

Ramos was digging himself deeper into a hole. Blackmail is no minor crime, but his behavior could pile more serious charges on him. If he were to kill a cop, his life would be over. Desperation can cloud one's sense of logic. I'd seen it before in felons trying to escape the law.

"I'd like to take a ride out there," I said.

"To what purpose?"

"I might get him to give himself up."

"What makes you think so?"

"We've got his girlfriend."

Briggs thought for a moment, then said, “I’ll phone ahead and let them know you’re coming. I’ll radio you their exact location.”

On my way out, Briggs said, “Keep your head down.”

I signed for an Impala at the motor pool and picked Danny up at the front entrance to the precinct building. On the way, I apprised him of the situation.

We headed for the address on the other side of the Hudson Chief Briggs had given us. The industrial complex was larger than a football field, composed of several enormous flat-roof buildings and enclosed within an eight foot high chain-link fence. There were New Jersey State Police and local area squad cars visible in every direction. Two officers were stationed at the gated entrance. From where we were, we could hear occasional shouts and gunfire in the distance. A barrel chested trooper with arms like truck tires approached my side window and asked what my business was. I showed him my shield and said, “Where here to see Captain Libretti.”

He leaned in my window and looked past me at Danny. Danny showed him his shield, and the trooper said, “Follow the road to the right. You’ll see the activity. Captain Libretti is on the scene.” Before I drove away, he said, “Keep your head down.”

His partner opened the gate, and we rode into the melee.

The tableau appeared before us after we took the right and drove a short distance. We saw a large rusted warehouse surrounded by armed SWAT officers crouched behind police vehicles, wearing Kevlar vests and helmets. Their weapons were aimed at the front entrance of the warehouse. There was a large overhead door and a small entrance door to its right. A row of dirty windows ran the length of the facade on the lower floor. A police negotiator was positioned behind a vehicle pleading with Ramos through a bullhorn. His words fell on deaf ears or were answered with a single gunshot.

I parked a safe distance away, and we walked toward an armored SWAT vehicle, which they were using as their command center. Several uniformed brass were standing with Libretti as we approached.

Captain Libretti was short and stout, with an enormous belly that screamed—too much pasta! By the amount of gray hair that protruded from the sides of his hat, I took him to be mid-fifties. His loose jowls were almost bulldog looking. He finished his conversation, then turned to us. Danny and I gave him a salute, which he returned. I said, "Detectives Graham and Nolan from the 35th."

"Chief Briggs told me you'd be coming," he said. "But he didn't explain *why* you'd be coming."

"Our department wants Leon Ramos in connection with blackmail and a possible murder charge."

"I'm aware of that, detective, but what do you think you can do that *we* can't do?"

"I might convince him to give himself up."

"We have a negotiator on the scene," Libretti said.

"But you have nothing to bargain with," Danny said.

"And what have you got," Libretti said?

"We've got his girlfriend in our lockup," Danny said.

Someone shouted in the distance, and a shot rang out in response.

"This guy's taking potshots at my officers," Libretti said. "He has no qualms about killing one of them. And he won't talk. If one of you can pull it off, then have at it. But if you can't budge him, I'll send in my SWAT team."

Danny said, "What kind of gun did he grab?"

Libretti said, "Glock 19, Standard issue."

"Why not wait for him to run out of ammo?" Danny said. "He's only got fifteen rounds, and he's fired off at least half."

"We've been dealing with this guy for hours," Libretti said. "I'm not waiting for him to take out one of my men."

With a signal from Libretti, an officer opened the rear doors of the SWAT vehicle and brought a vest over to us. Danny looked at me with an expression that said, "You or me?"

I was sure Danny would have accepted the challenge without hesitation and handled it well, but my paternal instinct kicked in and I felt an unwarranted need to keep Danny out of harm's way.

I slipped into the vest and said to Danny, "Seniority over enthusiasm."

Libretti said, "No closer than where the negotiator is."

I crouched low and walked toward the negotiator. With another hand signal from Libretti, the negotiator waited for me to reach him, then handed me the bullhorn. He stepped back as I leaned across the hood of a police unit and brought the bullhorn up. "Leon Ramos," I said. "This is Detective Graham from NYPD. Can we talk?"

I waited for a reply.

None came.

I tried again.

"I have a message from Samantha," I said. "She wants you to come back to her, give yourself up."

The surrounding activity had quieted down. It was silent inside the warehouse. I lowered the bullhorn and looked back at Captain Libretti. He was watching me with a look of dissatisfaction and impatience.

I brought the bullhorn up again and said, "If you come back with me, we can work this out. Samantha believes we can. She told me you wouldn't leave her holding the bag. She said she'd be waiting for you."

Leon Ramos' voice boomed from a small window beside the front door. "I'm not going to jail," he shouted. "Samantha can think whatever she wants."

Ramos wasn't saying what I'd hoped he would say, but at least he was talking.

"I'm offering you a chance to make things better for yourself," I said. "I promise you a fair trial for your charges, but if you kill somebody today, you'll go to jail for the rest of your life. I'm offering you your best and last chance for help," I said.

"Go back where you came from, detective," Ramos shouted. "I don't need any promises."

A gunshot that pinged off the vehicle's hood inches from my head followed his ill-fated advice. A second shot struck the bullhorn and knocked it from my hand. When a third shot whizzed by my head, I threw myself to the ground. I squeezed into a fetal position as another shot hit the pavement close by. Ramos had me pinned to my position. I couldn't stay where I was. I had to get to cover out of his line of fire. I stayed low and ran to the front of the warehouse, and pressed myself against the wall. Ramos left me no choice but to confront him or try to escape to safety. Trying to run for cover through the lot would make me an easy target. I was wearing the Kevlar vest, but the vest wasn't a suit of armor. There are vulnerable areas not protected by the vest that would be fatal if struck by a bullet.

There was almost complete silence among Libretti's officers. I was sure he'd ordered them to stand down because of his concerns for my safety.

As I inched along the building toward the front door, I saw Danny, with his gun in hand, run across the lot to the far corner of the building and disappear around to the rear. The front door wouldn't budge when I tried to open it. Maybe Ramos had locked it from the inside. I made my way down the side of the building and found a single door. The door was unlocked. I opened it and squinted through the darkness. The warehouse was in heavy shadow. I pushed the door back further and crawled inside on my hands and knees.

I removed my gun from my hip holster and released the safety. My standard carry was a Colt Defender. I had auditioned many handguns, including 9mm and .38s. Although the Colt was cumbersome because of its size and weight, I felt comfortable with its larger caliber. It had saved my life more than once. I didn't know where Ramos was, and I wasn't taking chances.

The only light came from the row of dirty windows to my left, facing the open parking lot. They looked like glaring eyes staring into the darkness. I closed the door behind me and stood in the quiet, waiting for my eyes to adjust to the darkness. The occasional sound of a rat's nails tapping on the cement floor as it scurried through the darkness broke the silence. I could hear the rhythmic sound of dripping rainwater in the distance. Through the shadows, I saw wooden crates and barrels stacked at various locations. Some were tiered as high as the ceiling; others were only two tiers high. There were abandoned cubicles and shattered glass partitions placed about the floor amongst several pieces of large dismantled machinery. Winches and tangled chains hung from ceiling rafters like snakes dangling from tree branches in a tropical jungle. Ramos could've been hiding anywhere in this maze of confusion. Self-preservation told me to find my way out to safety. My ego told me to find Ramos.

From where I was, I saw three opened windows. Two were near the front door, and one was at the end of the row. Ramos had to be beside one of the opened windows so he could fire out at his pursuers. He may have seen me enter the building. If he did, he'd be ready for me.

I wondered where Danny was or if he'd gotten into the building. If he had, it made the situation riskier. A shot fired for the wrong reason could prove fatal to its unintended victim.

I moved deeper into the warehouse, being careful where I stepped. I kept my gun at my side and used my free hand to feel my way where there wasn't enough light to see. I moved closer to the windows where Ramos was likely to be. As I did, I saw Ramos' silhouette run in front of the windows toward the last window in the corner of the room. I stood where I was so as not to give away my location. At least I knew where Ramos was. I inched my way closer to the window, my eyes darting in every direction, looking for movement in the shadows. When I got closer, I discovered a single row of boxes running parallel to the windows, creating a dark corridor. There was total darkness beneath the windows. Ramos could be crouched down under any of them, waiting for me. I bent low and walked behind the boxes, eyeing each window through the spaces between each box. I counted each window as I passed, but didn't see Ramos. There was but one window left. I moved away from the boxes, being careful to keep out of the window light. As I did, I heard a sound behind me. Before I could react, a shot rang out, filling the darkness with a blinding white flash. I threw myself to the floor and scampered behind the boxes.

Ramos had found me before I found him.

I crawled along the floor to the other end of the boxes. When I looked back, Ramos was squinting into the shadows where he had just fired, Pivoting his gun hand from left to right, looking for his next shot. I watched him step around the end box and walked along the row of boxes toward me. I stayed low in a shadow and watched his silhouette as he moved closer.

As I waited for Ramos, my eye picked up movement in the shadows to my right. Danny Nolan had stepped out from the darkness into a beam of pale window light. He was searching for me. He didn't know Ramos was on the other side of the boxes. Bath in the window light; he had presented himself as a perfect target. If Ramos saw him first, Danny was a dead man. I couldn't shout out to Danny without giving up my position. But I couldn't let him take a bullet from Ramos, either. I had to think fast. My mind was reeling. I couldn't think of anything that would abate the deadliness of the situation.

I waited and hoped for the best as my eyes darted from Danny to Ramos. I watched Danny walk along the boxes toward the other end, while Ramos continued toward me. Both men were deliberate and cautious as they moved through the darkness. Both were searching for me, but for different reasons. If they surprised each other in the dark, one of them could die. I had to make a move now!

My eyes followed Ramos as he inched his way through the shadows in my direction. When he walked into a patch of window light, I shouted, “Give it up, Ramos!”

He pointed his gun at the sound of my voice and fired. I dropped onto one arm. Angled my gun up and took a shot. My .45 slug slammed into his chest, throwing him back into the stack of boxes. The boxes tumbled to the ground, and he went down with them.

Danny ran around the end of the boxes with his gun out in front of him and dropped onto one knee. He saw Ramos lying still under the pile of boxes, and spotted me on the floor. He stood up and holstered his gun. “I didn’t know where you were until I heard the shots,” he said. “Are you okay?”

I nodded as I got to my feet.

“What about him?” I said.

Danny kneeled over Ramos and felt for signs of life. “He’s dead,” he said.

I walked to Ramos and looked down at him. It wasn’t the first time I had to kill another human being. Living with a killing is never an easy thing, no matter how justified.

I said, “Ramos threw away the last chance I offered him.”

Danny said, “His girlfriend will wait for him for a long time.”

CHAPTER 32

On Friday afternoon, at the behest of Chief Briggs, I assembled the principals of my investigation at the office of Hayden Benning. Briggs wanted my final report of the case to be complete in every detail. Including evidence, testimony and personal opinions of each principal involved whether guilty or not. I wasn't to leave out any detail, no matter how insignificant I may have thought it was. Briggs wanted no backlash from the Mayor or the city council. Although we had done the footwork, he had taken the mental pounding from the city administrators. We had worked hard and long on this case and he wanted it put to rest.

I'd hidden a digital recorder and microphone behind a set of books on a shelf by the office door. Since the moonlight murders were a high-profile case, Briggs insisted we make an audio recording "to cover our asses" should there be inquiries before, during, or after the trial. I suggested it was a bit too "James Bond." He said, "It works for Bond, it'll work for us."

I'd gathered enough information to reveal the who, how, and *why* of the Moonlight case, and was ready to give Chief Briggs the final report he expected. There was also enough evidence to charge the abductors of Ruth Ellison. The additional facts Greasy John provided me relevant to each player in my case, filled the cracks and helped bring the case to a close. Armed with that info, I was ready to make arrests and name the murderer.

A light rain beat against the window glass that looked out over Fifth Avenue. Clouds wrapped themselves around the city like a soft gray blanket, denying the sun its job and stifling the populace with weighted air and an overabundance of moisture. Despite the bad weather, everyone I had summoned showed up.

Ruth Ellison was sitting in an upholstered folding chair by the front windows. She had recovered from the trauma of her abduction and was putting her life together. When our eyes met, I gave her a reassuring look. She offered me a dubious smile as if she had no right to display joy until she received the closure she had been seeking. I hoped the conclusion I was about to offer her would be the catalyst for her new, happier life.

Hayden Benning sat behind his desk, tapping a metal letter opener on his desktop in a display of nervous anticipation. Andriana Blanchet was in a chair beside him. Her beauty couldn't disguise the consternation on her face.

Samantha Evers didn't look happy seated on the end of the sofa. She hadn't much to be happy about, awaiting trial on blackmail charges. She wore a gray sweatsuit and matching workout shoes. A black headband held her hair back. She looked like she'd just come from a gym. Her emerald green eyes seemed to have lost some of their luster. Despite having lost her lover, I saw no signs of mournfulness.

Charles Blanchet and his sister, Nadine, arrived together. Charles was out on bail, awaiting a trial on a charge of assault and battery. His girlfriend's condition hadn't improved. If she succumbed, he'd face manslaughter charges. If he *or* his sister conspired to commit murder; that would up the ante. They sat on a two-seater sofa, looking annoyed and indignant. Charles wore tan khakis and a blue cardigan sweater. His sister was wrapped in a tight black dress that she might have fit into when she was twelve. When she crossed her legs, the hemline rose well above her knees.

Charles Blanchet said, "Why are *we* here, Graham? We've committed no crime."

"Today we'll see who committed crimes and who didn't," I said.

I had stationed Danny Nolan by the office door with two uniformed officers, Patrolman Merrill and Sergeant Whitlock. Merrill opened the door at the sound of heavy rapping, revealing a grumpy-looking George DeMarco. DeMarco walked in with an unlit cigar in his mouth. The three-piece suit he wore made a difference in his appearance from the times I had seen him earlier. As he walked toward me, he said, "What is this, Graham? I thought I was through with this Quinlan thing."

"Have a seat, big shot," I said. "You'll find out."

DeMarco walked to a leather armchair, unbuttoned his jacket, adjusted his cigar in his mouth, and sat.

Above the whispered conversations in the room, I said, "We are waiting for Miss Allan."

"Why have you brought us here, detective?" DeMarco said.

"To satisfy all of your curiosities," I said. "And explain how the investigation came to its conclusion."

"I don't have curiosities," DeMarco said. "I didn't commit any crime."

"That's why we're here," I said. "To expose who *did*."

"Are we *all* under arrest?" Samantha Evers said.

She asked sarcastically and offered a wry smile to the others in the room.

I said. "You've already been arrested once. If you're convicted of a crime, a jail cell and an orange jumpsuit will improve your appearance *and* your cavalier attitude. I suggest you sit and listen to what I have to say."

She didn't like my answer and her face showed it.

All eyes turned when patrolman Merrill opened the office door, framing Ashley Allan in the doorway. She strode into the room, looking flustered. "Sorry I'm late," she said. "Traffic was unrelenting."

I said, "We're about to start," as I directed her to an armchair at the end of the sofa.

She thanked me with a smile as she wiggled out of her wet raincoat and took her seat. The white pantsuit she wore over a pink blouse and the red pillbox hat resting delicately on her head made her look almost juvenile.

I walked to the center of the room and began: "I've asked you here because you are all an integral part of my investigation into the murders of the moonlight ladies. You are all connected in some way with the case. Either by guilt, coincidence or circumstance. With hard work and diligence, the NYPD has brought the case to a satisfactory close."

"You mean you're accusing one of us of murder?" Charles Blanchet said.

I ignored his question as I moved closer to Hayden Benning's desk. I directed my words toward him but avoided direct eye contact. "Although the killing of the moonlight ladies was the prime focus of our investigation. There was a second crime uncovered, just as heinous and even more callous."

All eyes were on me with cautious curiosity as I turned to face Hayden Benning. "I'm referring to the murder of your partner," I said. "Mike Ellison."

Benning's face became a combination of surprise and brashness. "Mike took his own life," he said with angry certainty. "The inquest proved it."

"Further investigating proved otherwise," I said. "It proved you murdered your partner."

Benning sprang up from his chair. His face flared with anger and surprise. Merrill and Whitlock moved toward him, but I stopped their advance with a hand signal. There was a moment of tension while we waited for Benning's next move. The rhythm of rain pelting the windows broke the stillness in the room. Behind me, I heard a unison of heavy breathing.

"Sit down, Hayden, or you'll make things worse for yourself," I said.

Benning looked at me, then at the officers. Realizing the vulnerability of his situation, he eased back into his seat.

"We have transcripts of your phone calls to your wife and accomplice before the murders," I said. "It seems your wife was having second thoughts about committing murder. It became necessary for you to convince her it was in the best interest of you both to do away with your best friend. We also have the testimony of Miss Allan, who overheard your revealing phone conversation and brought that information to me."

I removed the list from my pocket we had found at Charlies Blanchet's apartment and handed it to Adrianna. She looked at it without comment.

I said, "We found that list under the mattress in your bedroom at Greenwich street. Why was it there?"

"I've never seen it before," she said. "Maybe it belongs to Charles or his girlfriend."

"It belongs to you," I said. "Yours were the only fingerprints found on it."

Adrianna Blanchet lowered her head. She appeared lost and defeated. The dream she sought was crumbling, and she knew it. "I made the list," she said. "When the murders began, I was afraid I might be next. I kept the list looking for a pattern, wondering why those women were chosen. Hoping each murder wouldn't bring the killer closer to me."

"Why would you think you'd be the next on the list?"

"I was the interloper. The deceiver. The one that upset the apple cart. I didn't know who was doing the killings or why. Perhaps guilt made me think I would be eliminated, too."

"Your phony phone call to me expressing fear and concern for your former husband and his sister was designed to cast guilt on them. It didn't work."

"That's just like you," Nadine Blanchet said, with as much disdain in her tone as she could muster. "Charlie has always been fair to you, even after the divorce. But it didn't matter to you. You were always a self-serving person."

Samantha Evers looked at her sister and said, "Good God, Adrianna."

Adrianna looked at her husband and said, "I told you it wouldn't work. "

Benning snapped back, "Keep quiet!"

I turned back to Benning. "You were the only person who knew I was investigating the death of Mike Ellison. I mentioned it to you that day in your office. Fearful of the consequence, you delivered a threatening letter to Ruth Ellison, hoping to dissuade her from continuing the investigation into her husband's death. When that didn't work, you plucked Kagan from a group of homeless and promised him money if he'd break into Mrs. Ellison's home to scare her into submission, which didn't go as planned. Your third attempt was out of desperation. You abducted her, hoping that would convince me to give up the case. You recruited Lester Kagan to do your dirty work. Your plan wasn't to kill Mrs. Ellison, so you had Kagan bring her food and water until you hoped to hear from me. When I agreed to drop the case, you were about to release her, but we found her before you could."

I looked over at Ruth Ellison but directed my words to Benning, "You put that woman through hell," I said, "and you're going to pay for it."

"You can't prove any of that," Benning said.

"You're a clever business owner but a poor criminal," I said. "Although your warning letter was clean of evidence, you left a single thumbprint on the envelope. An amateur mistake that'll put you behind bars. With that evidence and the statement we secured from Lester Kagan, I'm sure the AG will put the pieces of the puzzle together and bring charges accordingly."

"You have no motive," Benning said. "Why would I kill my partner?"

"Insurance records show you and Mike took out life insurance policies, naming each other as beneficiaries. It included an addendum that turned over full ownership to the surviving partner. The escort service was on shaky ground then. With Mike out of the way, you stood to gain one hundred thousand dollars and become sole owner, allowing you to make moonlight ladies successful. I'd call that motive."

I nodded to Merrill. As he approached Arianna Blanchet, she stood and put her wrists behind her, accepting her new silver bracelets. I'm sure they were the most nondescript piece of jewelry she'd ever worn. She would find none of that fashion and opulence where she was going.

Whitlock removed his cuffs from his belt and stepped closer to Benning. As he did, Benning snatched the letter opener from his desktop, grabbed Adrianna Blanchet around her waist, and pulled her against him. She screamed as he pressed the tip of the opener to her throat, then prodded her toward the office door. "Get back or I'll kill her!" he said. No one moved. I put my hands in the air to mitigate any confrontation. The officers took my cue and stepped away. Benning maneuvered his wife toward the door, his eyes darting in every direction, his face flush with fear and desperation.

Danny was still at his post by the office door. As Benning moved toward him, he said, "Out of the way, detective." I waited to see what Danny's next move would be. I was sure he would step away from the door to defuse the situation.

Danny didn't move.

Danny's eyes locked onto Benning's. You could hear the hush in the room as everyone waited to see what either man would do next.

Benning took a step closer to the door and said, "Move away!"

Danny reached down and calmly turned the key in the door lock. "You're not going anywhere," he said.

Benning's eyes widened. He said, "Unlock it or I'll cut her."

Danny stepped closer to Benning. "No, you won't," he said.

There was a stretch of silence between the two men. Benning's eyes moved around the room like a caged animal, trapped by the simple turn of a key.

"I'm warning you," he said. "Get away from that door!"

He pressed the point of the opener hard against his wife's throat. Danny was quick. He slapped the opener out of Benning's hand and threw a right into Benning's jaw. Adrianna screamed as the opener clattered to the floor and Benning followed it down. Danny kicked the opener away and lifted Benning to his feet by his shirt front. But Benning wasn't through. He shoved Danny away, rushed to the door, and took hold of the key in its lock. Danny grabbed Benning's hand and held the key in its place. A contest of strength ensued as Benning tried to turn the key while Danny held it fast. Officer Whitlock came up behind Benning, yanked Benning's free arm around behind him, pulled him away from the door, and snapped on the bracelets. Danny turned the key in its lock and opened the office door, then stepped back in a gesture of mock courtesy. As Benning and his accomplice wife were escorted out the door, he looked back at me. "You'll regret this, Graham," he said. "I've got connections and money."

I regarded his words as a threat he could ponder in his prison cell for the rest of his life.

No one spoke as I walked back to the center of the group. When I looked at Ruth Ellison, she was dabbing her eyes with her handkerchief. I tried to show her another smile, but she avoided my look.

DeMarco broke the silence with, "Guess that answers one question. Kidnapping *and* murder. Those two won't see daylight for a long time."

Samantha Evers said, "I can't believe my sister would do a thing like that."

"That's the same thing she said about you," I said.

"Did those two kill the moonlight ladies, too?" Samantha Evers said.

"The moonlight murders are a separate crime," I said.

DeMarco said, "If we're the only ones left in this room, then one of us is a murderer. If they didn't kill the moonlight ladies, who did?"

I scanned the faces in front of me. Each displayed feigned innocence, anxiety, or indifference. All awaiting breathlessly to know the identity of the killer of the moonlight ladies.

One of them already knew.

Ruth Ellison, in her seat by the windows, was twisting her handkerchief between her fingers in a display of uncertain anticipation. When our eyes met, she turned her face to the windows. I wondered if she had responded that way out of a sense of embarrassment, or perhaps—untold guilt. She had gone through a lot during the investigation and was experiencing a roller coaster ride of emotions.

George DeMarco chomped on his cigar like it was a licorice stick. He pulled it from his mouth, examined it, then poked it back in again, repeating the process several times. He looked like a man worried about spending the rest of his life in prison.

Ashley Allan sat with her hands folded in her lap, listening like a schoolgirl on her first day of class.

Unmoved and impatient, Samantha Evers waited for an answer.

DeMarco said, "Say it, Graham! Don't keep us hanging!"

The air in the room was stagnant with curiosity. I stepped closer to Ashley Allan and said, "Thanks to Miss Allan's courage and cooperation, we were able to secure enough evidence to prove Mr. Ellison did not commit suicide. Although the crime was committed three years ago, through hard work and diligence, we were able to identify his killers."

Ashley offered a self-effacing smile. I looked at her directly and continued. "Additional evidence concludes beyond a reasonable doubt that—" I paused for a millisecond, which seemed like an eternity as I struggled with what I was about to say. I was looking at a face I'd believed in. A face of innocence that had looked to me, seeking sympathy and understanding. A face that would not exist after today. The words came hard for me, but I continued without hesitations or misgivings. "—you, Miss Allan, are the killer of the moonlight ladies."

Samantha Evers shouted, "Holy crap!"

Ashley Allan sat up in her chair, her eyes wide, her face flush with surprise. "That's ridiculous. I have no reason to kill anyone."

Samantha Evers said. "Makes sense. A secretary knows more about the business than anyone else. You had access to information no one else had."

I gave Ashley time to respond. When she didn't, I said, "And you used that information to commit murder."

"You had access to the dates and times of each escort," Samantha Evers said.

"Of course, I had that information. It's part of my job. Where's the crime?"

"The crime is in the systematic elimination of the moonlight ladies," I said. "A devious proposal you planned in your head to destroy the business by murdering innocent women."

"Why would I do that?"

"Vengeance,"

"Against whom?"

"A man you loved but who didn't return your love—Hayden Benning."

Ashley Allan's face turned hard; her nostrils flared. Her innocent beauty melted away like a spring snow. All eyes followed her as she walked to the windows and looked down onto Fifth Avenue. She stood listening to the sounds of the city below. She folded her arms over her chest and contemplated the patterns of raindrops snaking down the window glass. She was a woman, confused, angered, and thinking hard, trying to find the words to exonerate herself from a crime she knew she had committed. Without turning, she said, "It's true. I was seeing Hayden during the time he was starting the business." She removed a handkerchief from her pocket and dabbed her moist eyes to garner sympathy. "It didn't take long for me to fall in love with him. I thought I had found the man of my dreams."

"Until he hooked up with my sister," Samantha Evers said.

Ashley Allan turned and faced me and spoke like we were the only people in the room. "She was only after his money. I saw through her and told Hayden. He refused to believe me. Our relationship soured, and he ended it."

"That's when you became involved with Mr. DeMarco," I said.

Demarco sat up in his chair and said, "Hey! I don't know nothin' about a murder."

Ashley Allan walked back to her seat and sat. She said. "I don't know why I got involved with George. Maybe it was my way of getting back at Hayden."

"But you weren't satisfied," I said. "You watched Benning build the business to a profitable margin and gain the good life with Adrianna Blanchet. The hatred and jealousy burned inside you. The life of an escort was what you wanted. You desired to wear fancy gowns and pearls and fine jewelry. You longed to carry bouquets of roses and hold onto the arms of rich, well-bred gentlemen. But, another woman got the grand prize. All you got was a desk, a laptop, and a cup full of pencils."

"She took away my life with him."

"That's when you devised your plan to destroy him and his business," I said.

"I don't know nothing about this," DeMarco shouted from his seat.

"If I couldn't have him, no one could. I went to see him to beg forgiveness. I pretended to accept his situation, to make him believe there was no animosity between us."

"And he believed you," I said.

"I can be very convincing when I need to be," she said.

"You almost fooled this cynic," I said.

"Although we'd established a normal relationship again. He had refused to hire me as an escort."

"He threw you a bone by offering you the secretary position."

"I gratefully accepted it."

"Unwittingly he put you in a position to destroy him."

"I used all the resources I had."

"Which was to eliminate the moonlight ladies and Hayden Benning to satisfy your vengeance."

"This is sick shit," DeMarco said.

Samantha Evers said, "Why didn't you just"—she hesitated—"kill Adrianna Blanchet? Get her out of the way."

"Her feelings for Hayden Benning wouldn't let her," I said.

"How did you know it was her," Samantha Evers said to me, "and not one of us?"

"It was Miss Allan's own undoing," I said.

I turned to face Ashley and said, "That afternoon in your apartment when you put on a phony but convincing display of fearing for your life. You mentioned there had already been five murders, and you were fearful of becoming the next victim. NYPD had kept the fifth murder from the press. There were only a few people who knew about the fifth murder, other than myself, Chief Briggs, and Detective Nolan. The murderer would have been the only outside person with that knowledge."

A hush fell over the room until Demarco said to Ashley, "Looks like you bought the farm, lady."

Danny walked up behind Ashley Allan. As he removed his cuffs from his belt, I said, “She won’t need those.” Danny took Ashley by her arm and walked with her toward the office door. She turned and looked at me. A mask of confusion and self-pity had replaced her loveliness. It’s always a sin when the ugliness of evil conceals itself behind a display of innocence.

CHAPTER 33

I was sitting with Sandy on our usual bench at Oakwood Park. We had completed two laps around the lake and stopped for a breather. Sandy found the moonlight case intriguing and had been *interrogating* me to appease her jurisprudence curiosity.

"How could you be sure it was Benning that killed his partner, and it was Ashley Allan that killed the moonlight ladies?" she said.

"Fingernails," I said. "Each of the female victims had the same indentation marks on her neck. Mike Ellison had no marks on his neck, other than rope abrasions. Hayden Benning kept his nails manicured close. Ashley Allan kept her fingernails longer and fashioned for beauty."

"How did you know the marks on the victim's necks were made by fingernails?"

"The lab found a trace of keratin embedded in the indentations of Victoria Quinlan, the last victim. Human fingernails contain a substance called keratin. Although they didn't find keratin on the other victims, the markings on their throats were identical in size and shape."

"Why was no keratin found on the other victims?"

"Maybe the lab missed it or found no reason to look further. Doctor Geffkin told me, based on her experience, she believed human fingernails made the marks. The keratin proved her right."

"But how did you know the fingernail markings were Ashley Allan's?"

"I didn't. I had enough evidence to prove Ashley's guilt. The fingernails corroborated Doctor Geffkin's conclusion and cleared Benning of the moonlight murders. The lab found a partial print on the cigar we found at Quinlan's murder scene, but it wasn't DeMarco's. We had nothing to match it within the system. Until I remembered Ashley Allan had handed me a sheet of paper that day in Benning's office. When the lab checked the paper, her prints matched the partial found on the cigar."

"And she planted the cigar to further incriminate DeMarco," Sandy said.

"Exactly."

"Whose DNA was on the cigar?"

"It's inconsequential. She was careful not to leave fingerprints anywhere, but forgot about the cigar."

Sandy said, "Let's walk."

She took my hand, and we started a slow walk around the lake.

It was the best morning of the summer. The air was crisp. The sky was an unblemished blue. A gentle breeze swaying the tree limbs surrounding the lake also pushed the silken thread of Sandy's hair across her forehead. She swept them away with a whisk of her hand. I felt the best I'd felt in a long time with her hand in mine, sensing the love connection between us.

At the end of the lake, we stopped at the ice cream vendor. Sandy had strawberry swirl in a cup while I worked on two scoops of Rocky Road. We sat on a nearby bench.

"I'm glad you could help Ruth Ellison," she said.

"She had been right about her husband's murder, and finally received the closure she deserves," I said. "I'm sure now she can get on with her life."

"Why did Ashley Allan set up DeMarco for Quinlan's murder?" Sandy said.

"She saw Quinlan as her next easy kill. She knew of DeMarco's rocky history with Quinlan. DeMarco told me he'd dumped Ashley because she'd become too much of a baggage issue for him. He said she was kookier than those other moonlight ladies. When he dumped her, she set him up to take the hit for Quinlan's murder."

"Vengeance again," Sandy said. "And she staged that false break-in at her apartment to remove suspicion from herself."

"And the story she told me about her father abusing her was contrived. She was raised by both parents in a stable home in a small town near Albany, New York. Her father was the only caring person in her life. She made up the story of a boyfriend that had been killed to arouse my sympathy. She'd never had a romantic relationship with a man. That's why she became obsessed with Hayden Benning. What attention he paid her was enough for her to think he was in love with her as she thought she was with him."

"It must have felt like a new dawn to her," Sandy said.

"Until her love was unrequited. Then she hated Benning for abandoning her. And her hatred turned to revenge and then murder."

"She's a woman possessed by anger and retribution," Sandy said, "and suffers from a psychopathic disorder."

"How does evil conceal itself behind such beauty?"

"Beauty is no evidence of innocence," Sandy said.

"Somehow, I can't help feeling sympathy for her."

"You're deceived by her looks."

"I guess it's true," I said. "Beauty *is* only skin deep."

"Hell has no fury like a woman scorned," Sandy said.

Made in the USA
Monee, IL
18 December 2022